Michael

(Connelly Cousins, Book Three)

Abbie Zanders

This is a work of fiction. Similarities to real people, places, or events are entirely coincidental.

Michael

Connelly Cousins Book Three

First edition. February, 2016.
Second edition. September, 2019.

Copyright © 2016-2019 Abbie Zanders.

Written by Abbie Zanders.

All rights reserved.

ISBN: 1523979720
ISBN-13: 978-152397921

Acknowledgements

Cover design by incredibly talented Marisa at CoverMeDarling.com.

Professional editing by the incomparable M. E. Weglarz of megedits.com, a woman with a true gift for spotting plot holes, character anomalies, black holes, and other potential WTFs. Thank you, Meg, from the bottom of my heart.

And special thanks to some very special ladies – Deb B., Anjee Z., Carol T., Tonya B., Susan J., Perryne D., Carla S., Becky G., and Heather J. (and a few of you who prefer to remain unnamed – you know who you are) - for reading the first draft and making invaluable suggestions. This is a better story because of them!

… and THANK YOU to all of *you* for selecting this book – you didn't have to, but you did. Thanks ☺

Before You Begin

WARNING: This book contains alpha male characters: a badass biker, a sexy construction worker, and a brooding Army Ranger.

Due to strong language and graphic scenes of a sexual nature, this book is intended for mature (21+) readers only.

If these things offend you, then this book is not for you.

If, however, you like your alphas a little rough around the edges and some serious heat in your romance, then by all means, read on…

About this Book

Michael is the third and final book in the standalone Connelly Cousins Trilogy.

Many of you might recognize him from his occasional cameo appearances in my popular Callaghan Brothers series. That's because the Connellys are cousins to the boys in Pine Ridge, and live just over the river in the small valley town of Birch Falls.

If you're keeping track, Celina's mother, Erin, and the Callaghan matriarch, Kathleen, are sisters.

So sit back, relax, and come along with me for another visit to Northeastern Pennsylvania…

prologue

Michael

The old man is up to something, Michael thought as he lifted the mug of Irish coffee to his lips. Traditionally, the drink consisted of strong, hot coffee, a healthy shot of Irish whiskey, and sugar, topped with thick cream, but Michael preferred his without the sugar or the cream.

As was tradition, they'd gathered at the family-owned diner after the wedding reception had wound down. The newly married couple, Michael's younger brother Johnny and bride Stacey, had left long ago, but that didn't mean everyone else was ready to call it a night. His sister Lina was sitting in her husband's lap, laughing at something their Uncle Jack had said. The rest of the place was filled with Callaghan cousins from across the river in Pine Ridge and a few close family friends.

His grandfather, Conlan O'Leary, was smiling

along with everyone else, but the old man was preoccupied. Every now and then his grayish-white brows would knit and he'd look as if his mind was somewhere else.

Michael sat in the back, doing what he did best. Watching. Processing. Quietly observing. But once everyone else shuffled home with full bellies and bleary eyes, he called the old man out.

"Aye," Conlan admitted. "I've got a feeling."

Trained as an Army Ranger, Michael put a lot of faith in his instincts. A man's gut rarely steered him wrong, as long as he was smart enough to pay attention to it. In his grandfather's case, those "feelings" often proved eerily accurate, so when Conlan spoke, Michael sat up and listened.

"About what, *Daideo*?" The Gaelic word for grandfather rolled easily off his tongue; it was how he and his siblings had been addressing him since they first learned how to talk.

The older man thought carefully, as if deciding what and how much to say. "A lass," he said finally. "I think she's in some kind of trouble."

Michael raised an eyebrow, but the admission wasn't overly surprising. His grandfather had a soft spot for damsels in distress. Much of that might be attributed to the fact that he'd lost both of his daughters, one to illness and another – Michael's mother – to a plane crash. Or that out of ten grandchildren, only one (Lina) was female.

"Who is this lass? And what kind of trouble?"

"Someone who works for me, and I'm not sure. Like I said, it's just a feeling." Conlan rubbed his eyes and shook his head, looking weary.

Michael mentally ran through the female staff at O'Leary's Diner. Most of them were middle-aged and had been working there for a while, more like family than employees. His gaze found Meg, a forty-something who was blushing furiously and shaking her finger at something his cousin Ian had said. And Nancy, who was seventy if she was a day, bustling about with a pot of coffee in one hand and a bottle of whiskey in the other, refilling everyone's cups. Carly, Grace, and Tina appeared to be both fine and in good spirits, as well.

"Anything I can help with?"

Michael regretted the words the moment they passed over his lips. Conlan's gaze snapped up, his clear, green eyes fixing on Michael with triumph and approval. That weariness he thought he'd spotted only moments ago? Gone.

Yeah, he'd walked right into that one. Sometimes he forgot just how wily the old man could be.

"Aye, you're a good lad. Come back tomorrow night, around midnight."

"Midnight?" The corners of Michael's lips quirked. "Should I bring my cloak and dagger?"

Conlan didn't laugh. "She works the overnight shift."

"She's not here now?"

"No."

Which meant that whoever *Daideo* thought was in trouble was not someone he knew. Michael waited expectantly, but his grandfather said no more. "Is that all you're going to tell me?"

Another nod. "For now."

The short hairs at the back of Michael's neck began to prickle, never a good sign in his experience. When that prickling was followed by a tingle of foreboding chasing down his spine, he knew trouble was on the horizon.

He shifted slightly. "And just how do you think I can help?"

There was that green, laser-like gaze again. "Tomorrow, Mikey. Midnight."

Maybe he was feeling sentimental after the celebration, maybe he'd tossed back one too many, or maybe he was missing the rush of anticipation that preceded a new mission, but Michael found himself nodding his head.

"I'll be here," he confirmed.

By the next day, that sense of foreboding had only grown stronger. The more he thought about it, the more he was sure the feeling was rooted in something far more dangerous than a covert op: his grandfather was trying to play matchmaker.

It made perfect sense. The next generation was moving into the spotlight. His sister got the ball rolling when she tied the knot with Kyle. Then his cousin Jake over in Pine Ridge made things legal with his woman, Taryn. Johnny and Stacey upped the ante, not only jumping on the matrimonial bandwagon, but doing so while expecting their first child.

It was only reasonable to assume that Michael, the oldest of all the grandchildren, should be next. Then the old man could just sit back and wait for the brood of great-grandchildren. Family was everything to Conlan O'Leary.

That was fine – for *them*. But him? Not so much.

It wasn't that Michael had anything against marriage or family. He just couldn't see himself in that situation. He'd always been a restless sort and settling down in one place with one woman wasn't in the cards. It wouldn't be fair to her, whoever she might be. Eventually, he'd feel the need to move on, and then what?

Even now he was starting to feel edgy, the familiar pull gaining purchase. He'd been back in Birch Falls for nearly a year, the longest stretch he'd tread the same soil in more than a decade.

Though he had grown up here, he'd left right after high school to attend college and then med school, but ended up leaving during his residency. He enlisted in the Army instead, where his drive and intensity earned him a place in the elite Army Rangers. The constant travel and action suited him, but eventually he realized that he wanted something more than to be a lethal tool in someone else's hand. After returning to civilian life, he used his knowledge of the family construction business and his background in medicine to create a string of fitness centers that were franchising extremely well.

That's what had originally brought him back to his hometown—a joint business venture with his Callaghan cousins to open up a new place across the river in Pine Ridge. As an added benefit, he'd reconnected with his family.

Which was all great. But not *enough*.

Maybe his astute grandfather had picked up on that, and that was the reason why he'd asked for Michael's "help". To give him a reason a stay, if only for a little while longer.

He could have told him it was pointless. With the plans for the fitness center now finalized, his siblings happily married, and the wanderlust firing up again, it was only a matter of time before he left, in search of something *more*. Michael thought briefly about bailing, but he had given his word. And, to be honest, he was slightly intrigued.

So that night, promptly at midnight, Michael settled himself in the corner booth of O'Leary's Diner, the one reserved for family, expecting little more than a thinly veiled attempt to match him up with "a nice Irish girl." With any luck, it would be a quick meeting. He'd hear what his grandfather had to say, offer his solicited opinion, then be on his way back to the bar where the company of a very lovely and remarkably limber young woman awaited his return.

After that, well…

The place was nearly full. That wasn't unusual. As the only twenty-four-hour diner in the area, it was a popular stop for those who worked second shift in the blue-collar town, as well as those who'd just come from the late night flick at the movie theater down the street.

He surveyed the occupants with mild interest, again wondering what his grandfather was up to. Then his skin began to tingle; his senses rocketed into a state of alertness. He scanned again, looking for the source.

A small figure moved into view, drawing his attention. Her back was to him, but it didn't matter. Dark, cascading hair fell halfway down her back, escaping the attempt to contain it in a pink tie band. The simple pink and white waitress uniform could not hide the lush, full hips beneath the slim, curvy waist. Shapely, toned legs extended below the mid-thigh hem, legs that had been made for high heels.

The attraction was instant. And somewhat shocking in its intensity.

Michael sat up straighter. He knew, without a doubt, that she had to be the one his grandfather had been talking about.

She turned toward him then, working her way back along the row of booths with a coffee pot in hand. She had delicate features, a natural, carved-by-the-angels kind of beautiful. And when she smiled, it was like pure sunshine.

No wonder the old man liked her.

The server was closer now, only a few tables away. She offered another smile to the trio there (college students, by the look of them) then bent forward to refill their mugs. One of them, a young guy with a half-shaved head, couldn't tear his eyes away from gazing at her ample chest and Michael felt a sudden, powerful urge to gouge out those eyes and feed them to him.

"She's something else, isn't she?" Michael was startled by his grandfather's voice. Somehow the old man had managed to approach without him noticing. Michael gave himself a mental shake. All this downtime was making him sloppy. He was getting too soft, complacent.

Conlan O'Leary eased into the booth opposite his grandson, his bright green eyes dancing with amusement.

And then she was there. Her scent hit him first. Warm. Sweet. *Delicious*. His eyes closed briefly as he inhaled deeply, savoring. Just that quickly, blood rushed to his groin.

"Would you care for some coffee?" she asked, her voice just as soft and lovely as the rest of her.

Michael opened his eyes to find her looking at him expectantly, carafe in hand. Her practiced smile began to fade as his gaze bored into her. She shifted her weight slightly.

"Coffee?" she asked again when he failed to

respond.

Big eyes, an unusual shade of turquoise, narrowed slightly. He recognized it for what it was: Awareness. Caution.

The awareness? That was mutual. It was no longer just the hairs on the back of his neck tingling and standing at attention; his entire body was at the party now, too.

But the caution? He was used to seeing lust, hunger, and anticipation in a woman's eyes, but not fear. Suddenly his grandfather's "feelings" made a lot more sense.

She took one step back, and Michael's body leaned toward her slightly. His muscles tensed, ready to chase her down should she attempt to flee. Then he realized what he was doing and forced himself to tone it down.

"Forgive him, Bailey lass. He's not quite himself this evening." Conlan gave her a wink, easing some of the tension. "He'd love some coffee, as would I."

Her smile returned, but it was less certain than it had been a minute earlier. She leaned across the table to reach for the empty cup in front of him. His eyes never left her face. Her cheeks flushed under his intense gaze while she filled his cup.

"She makes her own special blend, you know," Conlan was saying, then added with a chuckle, "She won't even tell me what's in it."

Her eyes flicked nervously from one man to the

other. Obviously coming to the conclusion that Michael was incapable of speech, she directed her next question specifically to the older man. "Shall I bring him a menu?"

Conlan chuckled again, his eyes sparkling. "No, lass. Just bring us some of your homemade cinnamon rolls, if you would."

"Yes, sir."

With one last uncertain look at Michael, she hurried away. Michael once again had to will himself to stay in place, stifling the urge to pursue her. He watched her go until she disappeared through the swinging steel door into the kitchen. Only then was he able to breathe fully again.

"That was Bailey Keehan," Conlan said quietly. "She seems to have made quite an impression on you, Mikey."

Understatement of the year, that. No woman had ever grasped his full attention as quickly or as completely as she had. Anything, any*one*, who could test his self-control so effortlessly did not bode well for him.

"What are you up to, *Daideo*?"

The older man grinned. The twinkle dancing in his eyes made him look remarkably younger than his eighty years.

Bailey returned with two warm rolls, placing one in front of each of the men. Michael noticed her hands were shaking slightly and frowned. Had she been as unnerved as he? Or was there another reason she would not meet his gaze? The one thing he did know was that fear had no place on her lovely face.

His protective instincts came alive, along with others. With some effort, he steeled himself against the surge of his baser urges and demonstrated some manners instead.

"Thank you," he said.

She seemed surprised to hear him speak. Her eyes flicked toward his for just a moment before she quickly looked away, but it was enough to refine his earlier assessment. Now they held a myriad of emotions: curiosity, shyness, definitely fear, and a healthy dose of fire.

"Bailey," Conlan began, "allow me to officially introduce you to Michael Connelly. Michael, this is Bailey Keehan, our newest addition and maker of the finest cinnamon rolls you've ever tasted."

"It's nice to meet you, Michael," Bailey said out of politeness, already turning to leave.

On an impulse, Michael reached out for her hand. The instant his fingers made contact, the tingling along his spine grew in intensity. Lifting her hand to his lips, he brushed a light kiss to her knuckles.

"Pleased to meet you, Bailey."

Her slight intake of breath was audible as another pink flush burned across her cheeks. Blue-green eyes met his, holding for more than a heartbeat this time.

Conlan cleared his throat, breaking the spell, and she swiftly reclaimed her hand.

"Thank you, lass. That'll be all for now."

Looking embarrassed, she nodded and walked away. Michael did not fail to see how she lifted her knuckles up to her lips as she did so.

Ignoring the triumphant gleam in his grandfather's eye, Michael took a sip of his coffee and let his eyelids drift closed. Strong and hot, just as he liked it. He followed that up with a bite of the roll, nearly moaning as it melted in his mouth. The rich, decadent taste reminded him of her scent as he rolled it across his tongue.

"So what's the deal, *Daideo*?" Michael asked, licking away the last of the gooey icing from his fingers, unwilling to waste even a drop of the sweet goodness on a napkin.

"That's what I want you to tell me. Something's amiss. I'm sure of it. And damned if I'm not feeling the need to help her."

Michael took another sip of his coffee. He'd felt it, too, right along with a host of other things. In those brief moments, he'd sensed a decided wariness beneath that fragrant, coolly polite exterior.

"She's afraid."

"No doubt about it," Conlan agreed. "But it's more than that. Tell me you don't feel it, too."

Michael thought back to his sudden and violent urge to rip out the eyes of the man who dared to ogle her earlier. The same guy who was looking at her ass right now. He fought down the growl that threatened to rip from his chest, and forced his own eyes back to his grandfather.

"You want me to run a background on her?"

"No, I've already done that." Conlan's expression grew more somber as he leaned forward and lowered his voice. "And found nothing."

Michael's eyebrows raised. Flying under the radar was one thing, but everyone left a digital footprint somewhere – credit scores, purchase histories, school records. To not do so required decided effort, and that raised a big red flag.

"I pay her under the table, of course. Cash. She's renting one of my apartments over on Sparks Street. Insists on paying three months in advance – all cash – on a month-by-month basis."

"In other words, no records, no commitments." Leaning back, Michael's eyes returned to her, attempting to look at her objectively, which wasn't an easy thing. She had a tendency to keep moving, he noticed, never remaining in one place for long. Granted, the diner was busy, but that didn't explain the way she continually glanced around her, more alert and aware of her surroundings than most people.

"Exactly. I've tried getting her to talk to me, but no such luck. I'm hoping you'll have more success."

"What makes you think she's going to talk to

me?"

"Let's just say you've already gotten her to notice you, which is more than anyone else has accomplished," Conlan grinned knowingly. Michael felt a surge of pleasure, even though he also felt as if he'd just been had again.

"You want me to ask her out, see what I can find out?"

"No." Conlan shook his head.

That was surprisingly disappointing. "Then what?"

Conlan's eyes tracked her as she went back into the kitchen. "She's scared, Mikey. Give her someone she can trust."

Michael withheld a snort. His grandfather wanted him to be a fucking *friend*? He didn't do the friend thing, not with women.

"She has you."

He expected a smile out of the old man, but instead his grandfather turned worried eyes on him.

"Aye, that she does," he admitted. The intensity of his feelings flashed in those Irish eyes of his. "But I'm an old man in her eyes. She'll not come to me for help. Nor will she let her guard down easily, I'm afraid."

"What about Lina?"

"Lina's got enough to be getting on with," Conlan said firmly. "And she doesn't have the same kind of senses you do."

The hair at the back of Michael's neck prickled

again. He took it for what it was. A warning.

As much as he hated to admit it, his grandfather was probably right. While Lina had a big heart, she often failed to see the bad in anyone or anything. Some of that might be his and Johnny's fault; they did have a tendency to be a bit overprotective where Lina was concerned.

His eyes flicked back to the doors when Bailey reentered the dining area, plates in hand. Her mouth was curved in a smile, but the rest of her screamed *off-limits*. It would take more than a night or two to gain her confidence. And, if he was honest with himself, the idea of getting to know her better wasn't unpleasant. But doing so from the friend zone? That might be difficult, especially after that primal caveman shit a few minutes earlier.

On the other hand, it had been a while since he'd had to work for something, and the challenge might take some of the edge off of his increasing disquietude.

The thing was … danger had always been more of a draw than a deterrent.

Conlan pierced Michael with a compelling stare. "Do this for me, Michael."

Even if he hadn't already made up his mind, that would have sealed it. His grandfather rarely asked for anything, and the use of his given name instead of the usual nickname underscored the seriousness of the request.

Michael nodded.

"Thank you, son," Conlan said gratefully, clasping him on the shoulder as he stood. "I'll send over what little I've managed to pull together. Right now, I've got to get back to the kitchen. Stay as long as you want. And don't be a stranger."

Now that he'd committed himself and no longer in a hurry to leave, Michael sat back and simply observed. Body language and behavior revealed a lot about a person, often more than traditional means, though he would use those as well.

Underneath those delectable curves were some seriously toned muscles. She was coordinated, graceful, and moved with an economy of motion he could appreciate. That suggested she stayed in shape, and was a "planner" – not someone prone to impulsive or frivolous behavior. Neither of those things was worrisome, but that constant wary alertness, that was another flaming red flag.

And since he was observing, he didn't miss the way her eyes kept returning to him.

He had her interest. *Good*.

Michael dropped a few bills on the table and got up to leave, catching her gaze once more with a silent message: *I'll be back*.

chapter one

Michael - Eight Weeks Later

Michael leaned over the pool table, eyeing his next shot carefully, his body unnaturally still. In a move of fluid grace, his right arm drew back then forward, forcing controlled contact between the stick and the cue ball. He stood and looked away, grabbing for the long neck that awaited him at the table, knowing with certainty that the 8-ball was heading unerringly toward the far corner pocket.

"How the fuck does he do that?" Kyle asked, shaking his head in amazement. "What is that now, four complete runs?"

Johnny laughed, his flashing green eyes lively. "Poetry in motion, isn't he?"

"Fuck you."

Michael's words couldn't completely erase the satisfaction in his eyes, nor could they hide the slight curve at the corner of his mouth. The three men were hanging out at Tommy's, Birch Falls' favorite local hot spot, shooting pool and downing a few cold beers. The place was packed, as was usual on a Friday night, but there was always a table reserved for them in the members-only back room.

Two of them were brothers by blood, the third had become one by marriage. For an outsider, it would have been difficult to determine which was which. All three were well over six feet of hard, rippling muscle. Michael and Kyle shared similar long black hair, which they tended to wear loose when just hanging out; Johnny's was a bit shorter, featured multiple hues of gold streaked with copper and bronze, and had slightly more curl to it, especially when damp.

Michael and Johnny boasted flashing green eyes that sometimes gave the impression of glowing, while Kyle's were an icy, clear blue. Each was clean shaven, with a strong jaw and finely chiseled masculine features that instantly attracted feminine interest.

Apart from physical attributes, the men shared several other things as well. The hint of a dark, dangerous air about them; underlying currents of ferocity and passion, contained beneath a surface of self-control. Confidence, an overwhelming urge to protect that which was theirs, and a bond between them that extended beyond blood and friendship.

Johnny pursed his lips, made some kissy noises and grabbed his crotch. "Right here, big boy," he taunted, causing the serious line of Kyle's mouth to crack into a grin.

Kyle, an undisputed genius when it came to motorcycles, was married to Michael and Johnny's younger sister, Lina. He designed and built his own customs, as well as knew everything there was to know about any bike ever made. Even before he'd met Lina, Kyle and Johnny had been friends, running in the same circles and sharing a love of bikes.

Johnny had assumed ownership of the family business, Connelly Construction, which did very well in the small, predominantly Irish community and beyond. Recently married to Lina's college roommate Stacey, he was as happy as Michael had ever seen him.

"So, who is she, Mike?" Johnny teased. Kyle raised an eyebrow as he racked the next set and Johnny elaborated. "Mike's unstoppable when he's got a woman on his mind, aren't you, bro?"

Michael shot him a warning glare. The last thing he wanted to discuss was his love life — or lack of it.

Johnny chuckled. "Man, I'm going to enjoy seeing you fall when you finally find your woman."

Michael grunted and lined up the break, placing the cue ball off-center and too close to the bumper. It was more challenging that way.

A pretty young server wearing too much makeup brought in another round of drinks. She paused when she approached Michael, just like several others already had over the course of the evening. Michael wondered fleetingly if they were taking turns, because he hadn't seen the same one more than once all night.

"Busy later?" she asked casually, though her eyes were intense and focused.

He gave her a quick, dismissive glance. *Too young. Too perky. Too fucking eager.*

"Yeah," was his short answer.

It was clearly not the reaction she expected. She recovered and followed up with a well-practiced pout. She probably thought the extra tight Tommy's tee and the quick trip to the ladies' room to remove her bra and splash cold water on her nipples would have elicited a better response.

"You sure?" she asked, bringing her ample breasts into better view, pressing them against his arm. "'Cuz I get off at midnight, but I have a ten-minute break I can take any time."

Why is she still here? Michael fixed her with a hard look. "Yeah, I'm sure."

The pout turned real, and she seemed confused by his rejection. He moved toward the other end of the table to take his next shot. She finally took the hint and headed out of the back room quickly, ignoring blatant attempts by some of the other patrons to get her attention.

"What's with you, man?" Johnny asked, looking concerned. "Why don't you just give her a little lovin'? Sweet thing like that won't take long.

We'll watch your beer for you."

Michael flashed him a look. "Not interested."

Kyle let out a slow whistle. Johnny looked shocked. "Uh-oh. This cannot be good."

"What?" Michael demanded. More than a little annoyed with the turn the conversation had taken, he straightened to his full height and touched the stick to the floor.

Johnny shook his head from side to side. "This just isn't right, Mike. It's not like you to let an opportunity like that slide by."

"Too easy."

"Since when have they ever *not* been easy for you? Hell, you nailed half the girls at the senior high school the year you discovered why your dick got hard." Johnny's voice resounded with the worship of a little brother. "And that one had a great ass, Mike. What is that, the fourth or fifth you've turned down so far tonight? You're scaring me, man."

A strange sense of déjà vu washed over him. Hadn't it only been a few months ago that they'd played out this same scenario? Except that time, it had been centered on Johnny's uncharacteristic lack of interest, not his.

Michael's eyes flashed with impatience. "I wonder what Stacey would say if she knew you were looking at that girl's ass, Johnny." It was a low blow and he knew it, but he was in no mood for his brother's shit. His gut was humming, had been all week, a sure sign that something was about to go down.

Or maybe that was the build-up of sexual frustration from going so long without.

Johnny's face lost its humor immediately. "You know better than that."

The two brothers squared off across the pool table, their infamous Irish tempers rising perilously close to the surface.

"Let it go, Johnny," Kyle said quietly, studying Michael's face. As a general rule, Kyle refrained from getting between them, but he must have seen Michael's jaw clench and felt the tension rising fast. Whether it was the quiet tone of his voice or the mere fact that he spoke up, Johnny shut up. Sulky now, he turned back to the table and downed the rest of his beer in one long swallow.

Discreetly, Michael checked his watch again. It was nine-thirty, which meant Bailey's shift at the diner didn't start for another hour and a half. Normally he waited a couple of hours before heading over, but he was feeling unusually anxious. That sense of foreboding had been riding his ass all night and it set him on edge. He didn't want to wait any longer to see her, nor did he have any desire to pass the time with the local talent. Hadn't, in fact, for some time.

All thanks to Bailey Keehan.

She had managed to capture – and hold – his attention, no small feat. The fact that she'd managed to do so with little or no effort on her part? Even more so. She probably didn't even realize how those shy smiles, quietly spoken words, and stolen glances affected him.

Images of big blue-green eyes filled his mind, eyes that lit up and sparkled the moment he walked in the door, before she could hide them. Pretty pink lips, shiny with vanilla-flavored lip balm, offering a shy smile. Dark hair, pulled back away from her face, tumbling halfway down her back. More often than not, a few riotous strands broke free and fell over her forehead and framed her face, giving her a tousled look that haunted his dreams.

For eight weeks he'd been making appearances at the diner, and each time, she seemed to trust him a little more. They were at the point now where if it wasn't busy, she'd actually talk to him. It was all general stuff, nothing personal, but it was progress.

He pictured her now, in that pink and white waitress uniform, far sexier than the tight neon yellow T-shirt the server had been wearing. The skirt rose just a few inches above her knees, hardly daring, but teasing him with the curves it did show. It rested snugly, but not tightly, around a perfectly rounded ass that moved in a natural sway and left him breathless whenever she walked away from him. The V of her neckline showed the barest hint of lush, round breasts, breasts that didn't require any man-made help to enhance their fullness.

What had started out as a favor to his

grandfather had become something of an obsession. Every Friday night for the past two months, he'd frequented the diner, sipping strong black coffee in the back corner booth after Kyle and Johnny had gone home to their wives. Sometimes he stayed for a few minutes, sometimes he sat there for hours.

Watching. Waiting. And, despite a few carefully placed inquiries, learning little more than he'd known that first night.

There were two things he was certain of. One, his grandfather was right—Bailey *was* hiding from something. And two, the more he was around her, the more he wanted her to trust him with her secrets and her body. Oh, he *wanted* her.

Thus far, he'd made no attempt to talk to her beyond the Friday night sit-ins. Nor had he allowed her to see him away from the diner. He feared if he had, she'd get spooked and all would be lost. He could see it in the way she looked at him—cautious yet curious—and the way she held herself when she took his order, as though poised for instant flight. He was allowing her to get used to him, to feel more comfortable around him, before he took things to the next level: connecting outside of her safe zone in the diner. For someone as used to instant gratification as he was, it was proving to be a difficult task. But he knew, without a doubt in his mind, that it would be well worth whatever effort it took.

The harder the challenge, the sweeter the

victory.

Leaning over the table, Michael took another shot, a perfect bank that completed yet another run. Kyle groaned loudly.

Michael wondered where Bailey was, and what she was doing before her shift. He knew what he *wished* she was doing. It involved him, a bed, and that sweet little pink and white waitress uniform.

* * *

Bailey

Bailey Keehan sat on the far side of the bar amid the shadows of the last booth, sipping her drink and feeling out of place. Her companions—she couldn't really call them friends—were on the dance floor with what she had to admit were some pretty hot guys. She'd been asked to dance a few times herself, but had steadfastly refused, preferring instead to observe from the sidelines. Bailey was more comfortable in the shadows than she was in the center of a dance floor.

Coming here had been a mistake. Even if it was Alyssa's twenty-first birthday, she should have said no. It wasn't like they were friends or anything; they just worked at the same place. But Alyssa had been very sweet and helpful, and after repeatedly declining her invitations to go out over the past six months, Bailey hadn't had the heart to say no when

Alyssa practically begged her to celebrate her first legal foray into Tommy's.

The ice in Bailey's glass was completely melted, diluting the powerful Long Island Iced Tea she'd unintentionally ordered hours ago. The bartender heard "iced tea" and assumed she'd wanted the high-octane version, but drinking was something Bailey generally avoided. It wasn't safe. Alcohol dulled the senses as well as the brain, and staying alert was critically important.

She swirled the stir-stick around absent-mindedly, counting the minutes before she had to leave for her shift at O'Leary's. As it did so often these days, her mind wandered to Michael Connelly. A shiver ran down her spine just thinking about him, not out of fear, but something else entirely. Something Bailey wasn't used to feeling. A tingling ache that centered behind her navel and caused her to press her thighs together. The same one that had her nipples pushing against her silky shirt and made her wish she'd chosen the bra with thicker cups.

Michael Connelly might just be the sexiest man she'd ever seen. A face straight out of mythology, a living example of male perfection. Silky dark hair, eyes the color of pristine emeralds that she swore sometimes glowed when he turned them her way. Rich, full lips that quirked a lot, as if he was enjoying some kind of private joke. She got shivers thinking what those lips could do, especially in combination with those long, capable-looking fingers of his.

She wondered where he was at that moment, what he was doing. Other than his weekly visits to the diner, they hadn't crossed paths. Despite having spoken with him on several of those occasions (beyond the usual server-patron dialogue), she still had no idea where he lived or what he did for a living. Their conversations were generally light and non-personal, covering safe topics like the weather, local goings-on, and things like that.

While part of her wanted to know more about him, she didn't dare ask, not unless she was willing to offer the same information in kind.

She wasn't.

She couldn't.

Her life was far too complicated for anything more than the brief *tête-à-tête*s they shared, but she could dream, couldn't she? If she was ever able to pursue something beyond a bit of harmless flirting, she'd want it to be with someone like him. Michael Connelly was so easy to be around, even if doing so sent her heart into hammering sprints. For a couple minutes each week, she could forget about everything else and just pretend she was normal. A normal girl, living a normal life, talking with an extraordinary man.

Suddenly feeling anxious, as she always did when she thought about him, she rose from the table and took the remainder of her drink to the bar. It was almost time for her to leave anyway. She needed to head back to her apartment and get changed before her shift.

She scanned the dance floor once again, but she'd already resigned herself to calling an Uber. Hopefully, the two-car Birch Falls service wasn't too busy and one of them would be able to come right away. She reached down into her pocket for her cell, the familiar anticipation building. Only a few more hours and she'd get to see her dark knight again.

She'd really begun to look forward to Friday nights. He always sat in the same spot, and she could feel his eyes on her when he didn't think she was looking. His low, smooth, velvety voice stroked her nerves deliciously when he ordered, and he had a look about him that promised untold passion and fire if given the chance. There was something dark and mysterious about him, something excitingly *naughty* that drew her to him like a magnet. Yet he was always very polite, and had done nothing to incite the hot and steamy dreams she was having about him nearly every night.

There was something inherently powerful about him, too. Something dark and fierce and dangerous. Only a few weeks ago, a group of guys came in after what was obviously a bar tour, and were quite free with the lewd and suggestive remarks. One was even bold enough to grab her ass. Mr. O'Leary, the grandfatherly owner of the diner, kicked them out immediately. Shortly after that, she noticed Michael had disappeared as well. In town a few days later, she saw the man who had grabbed her. His right arm was in a cast extending from his shoulder to his fingertips.

Though she knew it was just a coincidence and the two events weren't related, she couldn't help fantasizing that her dark stranger had somehow appointed himself her protector. Her secret knight in shining armor. The thought made her smile.

"Now, what would make a woman smile like that, I wonder?" a male voice speculated from close by, breaking her from her reverie. "My money's on something naughty."

She looked up and her smile faded instantly. It was the same guy who had been turning up too often for it to be by chance. At first, she'd told herself it was simply coincidence. After all, Birch Falls was a small town, and it was a common occurrence to see familiar faces at the diner, the grocery store, the book store, and the post office.

But no other familiar face gave her the same icy, leaden ball of fear in the pit of her stomach that this guy's did.

Which only served to remind her why she'd come to Birch Falls in the first place.

"Excuse me," she said politely, and tried to step around him. He moved a step to the left to block her, then one to the right when she tried again.

"Where are you going, sugar? Not leaving so

soon?" he asked, his eyes a little too bright, a little too excited. He looked over in the direction from which she'd come, searching for anyone who might be watching. Unfortunately, no one was looking their way.

Bailey glanced longingly toward the main door, the one she'd have to navigate through the dance mob to get to.

"You're all alone tonight, aren't you?" His voice was quieter as his hand closed around her upper arm.

"No, I'm not," she responded, wrenching her arm away. "I came with some friends."

"I think they ditched you, sweetheart. You can hang with me." His voice was too smug, too knowing. How long had he been skulking around? Had he been watching her? Another chill ran down her spine. Her first mistake was coming out in the first place. Her second was allowing herself to be distracted.

She offered a small smile. "Sorry. Not interested," she tried.

He smiled, though it didn't quite meet his eyes. Her hopes for a quick and easy departure were dashed, though it had been worth a shot. She should've known better; she wasn't exactly the poster child for lucky breaks.

Outwardly, she aimed for annoyed aloofness. Inwardly, her mind was feverishly working out the best avenue of escape. Chances were, this guy was just a garden-variety creeper whose ego overshadowed his common sense, but taking chances wasn't something she did unless she had no other option.

Getting to the main door was possible, but progress across the crowded dance floor would be slow and ditching him would be difficult. And once she got outside, then what? With no car, no ride, and no one paying attention, she'd be a sitting duck, far too vulnerable.

No, her best bet was a distraction and a quick exit. Two fire emergency doors flanked the sides of the public bar room, but opening those would sound the alarm and bring the authorities, which was unacceptable. The only other option was the door at the far end of the bar, the one with a sign that read, "Private – Members Only."

As a plan began to form in her mind, she squared her shoulders and lifted her chin, decision made. "Not that it's any of your business, but I'm supposed to meet someone here."

He laughed. "I don't believe you," he crooned, leaning in closer.

"I really don't care what you believe," she told him, fighting against the rising panic. She could *do* this. Tommy's was a public place, and filled with decent, law-abiding citizens, people she'd seen in town and at the diner. She'd been in far worse situations and had come out all right.

She just needed to calm the hell down and

focus.

Bailey turned on her foot quickly, going in the only direction she could. Straight to the back room and the door marked *Private.*

With a deep breath, she pushed open the door and stepped inside, only to find herself in the midst of a room full of big, muscular types playing pool and shooting darts. More importantly, she spotted a brightly glowing EXIT sign on the far end that would be her salvation.

Maybe. If she could navigate the sea of mass and muscle between here and there.

The room grew silent as one by one, heads turned in her direction. She was just about to mutter an apology and make a break for it when she spotted a pair of familiar, glowing green eyes fixed right on *her.*

chapter two

Michael

Michael felt the telltale prickle at the back of his neck (and an accompanying ache in his groin) a few seconds before the atmosphere in the back room at Tommy's changed dramatically. Tension sizzled to life, the level of testosterone in the air shot into dangerously high levels. The good-natured jibes quieted along with the rest of the conversations as all eyes turned to the door that led to the public area.

He didn't have to look; he knew who it was. He had some kind of extra sense that alerted him whenever she was near. He didn't have to see her beautiful face or sinfully lush curves, smell her unique sweet scent, or hear her low, purring voice to know it was *her*. His dick knew. It was instantly hard and aching, straining toward her like a compass needle pointing north. He straightened, slowly, and like everyone else, turned his attention to the doorway.

His heart stuttered and his breath caught. She looked beautiful. Her dark mahogany hair was loose, tumbling in waves almost to her hips, catching the lights as if she'd commanded them to wrap around her. She wore a silky blouse tucked into a pair of black stretch jeans that hugged her curves like a lover. The turquoise blouse highlighted those huge blue-green eyes, outlined tonight with something dark and smoky. Three-inch spike-heeled, glossy black sandals with a web of fine silver chains crossed over her high arches gave just the briefest impression of bondage and sent the ache within him into an all-out burn.

He groaned inwardly. *What the fuck was she doing here?*

She stopped just inside the door with a brief "deer caught in the headlights" look that made her eyes all that much wider and turned every man in the room into an instant hunter. Michael fought against the tightness in his chest and the roaring in his head that was urging him to run across the room, toss her over his shoulder, and take her back to his cave until the only name capable of passing her lips was his.

Even from across the room there was no mistaking her fear. *Good*, thought Michael. She should be afraid. Women did not venture into this part of Tommy's unless they were serving – or hoping to service, as it were. Michael was not the only one to notice that she wasn't carrying a tray of drinks. *Damn it.* He did not want to have to kill these men. He'd grown up with most of them.

Her eyes scanned the crowd, and damn if they didn't get even bigger. The increasingly fast rise and fall of her chest suggested imminent panic. A tender little lamb among some very hungry wolves. Michael braced himself. This was going to get very ugly, very fast if he didn't do something soon.

Look at me, sweetheart, he commanded silently. *Look at me, only at me.*

Then she spotted him. *Thank God.* Those huge blue-green eyes locked onto his and everything changed. In the span of a few seconds, her spine straightened and the look of alarm changed to one of determination.

* * *

Bailey

Bailey felt a rush of heat roll over her. It was him! Michael Connelly, looking good enough to eat in a black button-down shirt and a pair of those well-worn blue jeans, his emerald eyes pinned directly on her.

Her dark knight.

There he stood, gloriously fierce and ready for battle, lance in hand. Okay, so maybe it was a pool cue, but she blamed the adrenaline racing through her system for coming up with that analogy.

No time for her Camelot fantasies now, though. She took a mental snapshot to recall later, much later. She had a creep on her heels, and first and foremost, she had to get away from him before she entertained any more distracting thoughts.

Her eyes flicked again to the exit then back to Michael, who stood between her and escape.

"Bailey!"

Her pursuer entered the room behind her, his face a mask of thorough irritation. The attention of the occupants shifted from Bailey to the man in the doorway, and the temperature in the room grew noticeably cooler. Two large men, one with Adonis-like golden hair and one who looked very similar to her knight, stood and flanked Michael on either side.

Apparently, these guys took their members-only privileges seriously.

The guy following her must have realized it, too. He reached out and grabbed at her arm. "This has gone far enough," he hissed. "Come on, *sweetheart*, we both know you're not meeting anyone here."

Bailey barely avoided his grip with a quick twist of her shoulders. Her hopes of slipping through without incident were practically nil, not with being the center of attention as they were. She looked again at Michael, at the tense set of his shoulders and the intensity of his eyes.

What she was about to do was probably going to end any future hope of seeing her knight again, but she could see no other choice.

With purposeful steps, she made a beeline for Michael, pasting what she hoped was a cheerful smile on her face and praying that her voice didn't crack.

"Sorry I'm so late. I thought we were meeting out by the bar."

She reached both arms up around his neck – a full body stretch for her – and attempted to pull him down to her. For a horrible moment he did not move, and she was afraid she had wildly overestimated her probability of success, but then she felt his arms close around her and his mouth captured hers.

Marble, that's what he felt like. Warm, hard, malleable marble. Sizzling bolts of energy radiated out from each point of contact, sending a rush of heat straight to her core. Bailey might have gasped; it would explain how Michael's tongue managed to glide along her lower lip and then tease hers. Strong, solid arms tightened around her, pulling her closer in an unspoken command to press more of her body against his.

God only knew how long the kiss actually lasted. Two seconds. Two minutes. A month. The moment Michael's lips touched hers, the rest of the world ceased to exist. There was only *him*, holding her, kissing her as if he really *meant* it.

She needed the strength of those arms, because every bone in her body suddenly went from solid to liquid, melting under the power of that kiss.

Apparently, those fantasies she'd been having for the past eight weeks had been spot on.

When Michael finally pulled away, there was fire in his eyes. He relaxed his arms, but continued to hold her as his gaze lifted toward the door. With her body still pleasantly buzzing, she turned and saw her pursuer glaring at her, his face contorted in anger. The entire room had gone silent, waiting to see what would happen next.

Bailey was wondering that herself.

* * *

Michael

"Maybe you didn't see the sign. This is a private room. Members Only." Michael spoke the words quietly, but that only added to the power behind them. He was not a man who uttered idle threats, and even a loser like the guy chasing after Bailey should be able to figure that out quick enough. Additionally, anyone who encountered the wrath of Michael Connelly would also fall into ill favor with the other patrons, as other men began to rise from their seats or set their cue sticks to the side.

Whether the outsider had had too much to drink

or an innate death wish, he didn't know, but it didn't matter. He'd ventured where he was not welcome, and thought to push his attentions on a woman who obviously didn't want them. And not just any woman. *Bailey*.

After a brief hesitation, the guy thrust his chin out defiantly and took another step into the room. "She's with me."

It was the wrong thing to say.

Michael's eyes narrowed as Bailey clutched him harder. She was afraid of this guy; that much was clear. And that made Michael very, very angry. Without even realizing he was doing so, he pulled her closer to him and ran his hand soothingly against her back. Those protective instincts he'd been keeping tethered ripped free with the sudden, fierce intensity of a bolt of lightning.

And then, he *knew*. Bailey Keehan was his *croie*. His heart. *The one*.

That realization explained a lot. It also changed *everything*.

Looking over her head, his eyes found the worthless piece of shit that had driven Bailey into his arms. Medium build, medium height. Unremarkable brown hair, brown eyes. The kind of guy who could blend into the woodwork, easily overlooked, except for the cruel gleam in his eye. Except now he'd gone and drawn attention to himself, and not the good kind.

Michael's mouth curved up in a smile that

could have frozen Niagara Falls. "Wrong. She is with me. And you should have listened the first time."

The man's face reddened, but as he looked around at the unfriendly faces, he had to know he was in hostile territory.

"This isn't over," he hissed.

His self-preservation instinct must have kicked in, too, because he turned and hauled ass into the main area of the club. On a hunch, Michael gave a slight nod to a couple of the guys closest to the door and they followed after him.

Michael returned his attention to the woman in his arms. The incredibly soft, fragrant woman who was warming him from the inside out. Her eyes were glazed and a bit unfocused; her lips still slightly parted, reddened, wet and swollen from his kiss. The side of his mouth curved into a little smile. He'd imagined her like this a hundred times, though the reality was even better than expected.

She wasn't in her cute pink and white uniform. Her outfit was quite tame by Tommy's standards, but it set him on fire all the same. The way her blouse opened just enough to give the merest suggestion of what lay beneath, especially now with her breasts pressed lightly between his arms. The way the collar exposed the delicate curve of her neck, a screaming invitation for him to put his lips there. He knew that the silk beneath his fingers wouldn't compare to the silkiness of her skin; that her ass would be just as firm and tight outside of those jeans as in them. And her hair. Her hair spilled around her like shimmering satin in loose wavy curls. He longed to get himself tangled in that hair.

All too soon she seemed to gather her senses and pull away. With an inexplicable feeling of loss, Michael allowed her to do so, remaining close enough to steady her if needed.

"Thank you," she whispered. "You may not realize it, but you have just rescued a damsel in distress."

A slow grin spread across his face. Oh yeah, he was up for playing hero. For her, he'd be goddamn Superman.

"Who was that guy?" The question came out casually enough, revealing none of the rage that boiled behind it.

* * *

Bailey

Bailey fingered the smooth cotton of his shirt. Lies had a way of getting complicated real fast, so she tried to stick with the truth whenever possible.

"I don't know his name," she said softly.

Michael's fingers flexed against her waist. "Why did he say you were with him?"

"I don't know that either. He tried picking me

up in the bar, but I turned him down."

"Is this the first time?"

"That he's approached me directly, yes."

His eyes narrowed, filling in the blanks for himself. "What about indirectly? Has he been stalking you?"

She felt the tension increase around Michael like an electrical field. His voice was low, little more than a growl, sending shivers down her spine.

She shrugged, neither a confirmation nor a denial, wrapping her arms around herself. She had no proof, only possibilities.

"Hey," she said, changing the subject. She shifted her weight slightly. Back toward him. "Coffee and rolls on me tonight, if you happen to make it in, that is."

His eyes searched hers. Glowing green eyes like a predator. Except she wasn't afraid. She found herself wanting desperately to be his next meal. Shaking herself free of those dangerous thoughts, she added, "You know, it's the least I can do, since you came to my rescue and all."

* * *

Michael

Now that he knew what she felt like in his arms, knew what it was like to kiss her, nothing would keep him away. But if she thought he was just going to let this incident slide, she had another thing coming. There was more to this situation than she was letting on; he felt it in his bones.

That guy, whoever he was, had something to do with whatever had her spooked and running scared.

"I accept. But I have something I have to do first."

His eyes went briefly to the doorway where the tool had been standing only moments earlier. He didn't worry that the guy had gotten far. Joey and Dave, both former MPs, wouldn't have allowed it.

He felt her hand press lightly to his chest, sending little bolts of heat zinging through him, right into his groin. He looked down into the deep blue green of her eyes.

"He's not worth it," she said quietly.

Michael smiled and pushed a stray curl from her forehead, but said nothing. They'd have to agree to disagree on that. The rat bastard's fate had already been sealed.

To the astonishment of the others, who had been watching with undisguised interest, Michael put his hand on the small of her back and gently guided her toward the back door.

"I'm going to see that Bailey gets to work safely," he told Johnny and Kyle with a meaningful glance. "Hold the game for me, will you?"

They immediately understood his message: *keep that bastard here till I get back.* The two men nodded, probably at a loss for words. They weren't used to seeing him get territorial.

Then again, they'd never seen him with his *croie*, either.

"You don't have to do this," Bailey insisted as Michael led her out to his Harley, eyeing the machine with wide eyes. "I can just call an Uber or something."

"Ah, what kind of knight would I be if I did not see to your safe travels?" He allowed the soft musical lilt of his ancestry to color his words as he held out his leather jacket to her.

In the glow of the streetlight, he could see the rosy blush seep into her cheeks. He couldn't help but wonder if other parts of her flushed with a healthy glow as well.

"Have you ever ridden upon such a steed before, my lady?"

She cast her eyes downward. "Nae," she said, with a shy smile that had his balls tightening. "Pray thee, I have not, brave knight."

He straddled the bike and gave it a solid kick start, offering her a grin as the low rumble purred beneath him. When she made no move forward, he held out his hand.

"Come," he encouraged.

* * *

Bailey

Bailey was rooted to the spot. What the hell was she thinking? Only a few minutes ago she'd thrown herself into his arms, and now she was actually considering climbing on the back of that gleaming black and chrome death machine with him? Had she taken total leave of her senses?

She was not, by nature, a reckless or impetuous person. She was well organized, intelligent, and purposeful. She did not climb on the backs of motorcycles with dark (albeit gorgeous) wild Irish men. It would be totally out of character for her. Kind of like throwing herself against a dark, gorgeous, wild Irishman in a bar to escape the man stalking her.

But oh, had she not thrown herself at him, she never would have known the wonder of his kiss, or the feel of all that delicious hardness against her. Now she knew exactly what people meant when they said "the earth moved." For her, it had tilted entirely off its axis for the duration of that kiss and even a bit afterward.

But a motorcycle? Why couldn't he have driven a Ferrari or a Lamborghini or a Bugatti or something safe?

She looked at him, so fierce and beautiful under the glow of the street lamp that it nearly took her breath away. When would she ever get another chance like this?

If nothing else, this evening's events were a much-needed reminder that it was time to move on.

The thought hurt, more than it usually did, all because of the dark knight willing to slay her dragons. If she didn't do this, she would spend the rest of her life wondering, *what if.*

chapter three

Michael

Michael watched her carefully, keeping himself as still and non-threatening as possible. For as passionately as she'd clung to him and returned his kiss only a few minutes ago, she was back to being skittish.

So close. Don't push. Come on, baby, take a chance.

He'd been blown away by her unexpected boldness earlier, but one look in her eyes told him how terrified she had been. That fucker would pay for scaring her like that; just like that cocky little shit who'd made a very poor choice when he decided to grab her ass in the diner a few weeks ago. Michael had broken six bones in that guy's hand that night, not to mention his arm for good measure.

Now, he forced himself to remain patient. If he could lay for hours in the desert without moving a muscle, he sure as hell could straddle his Harley for a few minutes to let her work up the courage to trust him. His heart did a somersault when she took that first step forward.

"Put this jacket on," he told her, "and climb up behind me." He saw the excitement flash briefly in her eyes, saw how she summoned her courage, and felt a surge of pride. She dutifully slid her arms into the buttery-soft leather, inhaling as she did so, though she hesitated beside the bike.

"I promise I won't let anything happen to you," he said softly, keeping his hands on the grips. He could encourage her, but ultimately, it had to be her choice.

Still tentative, she put the toes of her foot on the bar and swung her leg over gracefully, settling in behind him. The way she moved suggested that she had studied dance or ballet at some point, or perhaps even martial arts. So feminine, and so strong.

His arousal shot up another couple notches. She would be fluid grace beneath him, on top of him, beside him… He closed his eyes and tried to concentrate. He'd allow himself to fantasize later, when he didn't have the benefit of her body so close to his that he could feel her warmth soaking into him.

Unsure where to put her hands, she rested them lightly against his sides. Michael bit back a grin. How ironic was it that women usually had no qualms about putting their hands on him, yet this one – the one he ached to feel against him – seemed reluctant to do so?

"You're going to want to wrap your hands around my waist and scoot up real close," he said, forcing a neutrality into his voice he didn't feel.

Bailey followed his instructions to the letter, inching up until she was nestled snugly and her thighs pressed against the outside of his. His mind went blank for a few moments, at least until her arms slid around his waist and she held him firmly. He stifled the growl that tried to rip forth from his chest as her fingers splayed across his abs. An innocent embrace, yet one that rocked him to his core.

"Where do you live?" he asked casually. The question was for her benefit, to foster her fragile trust. He already knew, of course. He'd followed her home after her shift often enough, waiting until she was safely inside to take his leave. But she didn't know that. Nor did he want her to.

He didn't miss her hesitation. She had concerns about revealing that kind of information to anyone, and for a woman living alone, that was a good thing. But he wasn't just anyone. Surely, she sensed that by now, or she wouldn't have looked to him earlier when she felt threatened.

"218 Sparks."

Inwardly, he breathed a sigh of relief; it was another small step in the right direction.

Over the vibration of the bike he could feel her heart hammering against his back. When he eased the bike forward, she pressed her face into him and tightened her hold. He chuckled when they pulled up in front of her apartment building a short while later and she continued to grip him tightly.

He killed the engine and said softly over his shoulder, "We're here."

"So soon?" She sounded genuinely surprised.

"Yes. Wasn't as bad as you thought, was it?"

"No," she said, a smile spreading across her face. "It was … kind of exhilarating, actually."

She took care getting off the bike, dismounting as gracefully as she had gotten on. He felt the loss of her warm body acutely, suddenly reduced to just the feel of her fingers upon his shoulders, then nothing. Sliding out of his jacket, she held it out to him.

"Go ahead and do what you need to do. I'll wait here."

She looked at him questioningly with those big, round eyes. He noticed she'd used a little shadow around the lash line, a smoky deep turquoise that highlighted the natural flecks now sparkling beneath the streetlamps. He liked it. A lot.

"You don't mind?"

"Not at all." He looked at his watch. "What time does your shift start?" *Eleven p.m. to seven a.m. Tuesday thru Sunday. She had Monday nights off. Spent the time alone in her apartment, reading romance novels or working on her laptop.*

Again, the slight hesitation. "Eleven."

"Plenty of time, then."

"All right," she agreed with a slight nod. "If you're sure."

"I am." He grinned again. More progress.

Michael watched as she walked into her building, looking once or twice over her shoulder as if she expected him to disappear if she looked away too long.

When she was out of sight, he lifted the jacket to his face and inhaled. The warm leather and faded scent of his cologne mixed with another, a sweet smell that reminded him of gooey iced cinnamon rolls right out of the oven, a scent he now associated exclusively with Bailey Keehan. He didn't bother to stifle the groan that rumbled forth, his mouth salivating as he imagined satisfying his cravings in creative and intimate ways. The thoughts sent shudders of pure desire through him, and his throbbing cock ached against the confines of his jeans.

She wasn't ready for that yet, he reminded himself. Which meant he needed to think about something else before he did something stupid, like push too hard. He'd never wanted a woman as badly as he wanted Bailey, and now that he'd recognized who she was to him, his body vehemently protested holding back any longer.

But hold back he would, because this need he

was feeling was about more than just sex. This was about *forever*. Once they crossed that threshold, there was no turning back.

Like you could turn back now, a little voice inside his head mocked.

The phone in his pocket vibrated with an incoming message from Johnny. *Party's ready to start. Where are you?*

Michael's upper lip curled back in a half-grin, half snarl, imagining Bailey's stalker being held in the back room at Tommy's, awaiting his return amidst the unfriendly hometown crowd. He thumbed back. *Be there in a few. Save me some.*

When he looked up again, Bailey was coming through the doors in that cute little waitress outfit. Her face lit up when she saw he was still there, waiting in the same place. *Damn*. His balls tightened painfully.

Behave, he commanded.

She swung onto the bike, more comfortable with the process the second time around. She even seemed excited by the prospect of riding again. Michael took instant notice of the fact that her bare legs were now pressing against him, her dark jeans replaced by that modest skirt. Not conducive to riding long distances, perhaps, but it was only a short ride to the diner, and if she wasn't saying anything, he wasn't stupid enough to bring it up.

Her arms wound around him without coaxing as she scooted against him. He swallowed hard against the heat that seeped through his jeans. Her hands moved confidently against his stomach, and he could have sworn she had snuck a couple of quick, exploring touches in there, but he wasn't complaining.

"Ready, my lady?"

Her light, musical laughter sent tingles into his center. "I am indeed, good Sir."

He paused for a moment, soaking it all in, until her fingers flexed and her body shifted behind him, reminding him of his task.

The trip to the diner was woefully short. He briefly considered circling the block a couple of times to extend the ride, but thought it best to save that for another time. Judging by the way she seemed to be enjoying herself, the offer of a long, weekend ride might go over well. He filed that away for later.

* * *

Bailey

Bailey kept her head up and her eyes open, determined to experience more of the ride this time. Now that she knew what to expect, it wasn't nearly as scary. Michael handled the bike expertly and holding onto him as she was, was a treat in itself.

Not only that, but when she was with him, she felt safe, as if nothing bad could happen when he was around. It was the same each time he came into the diner. For that hour or so, she breathed a little easier, knowing he was there, feeling his presence. *Safe*. When was the last time she'd felt completely safe? She couldn't even remember.

Under normal circumstances, she might have seen it as a promising beginning to something more, but there was nothing normal about her circumstances, and pretending otherwise wasn't going to do either of them any good.

This evening had been a grim reminder of exactly what could happen when she let her guard down. What if that guy wasn't just a small-town stalker, but another private investigator hired by Simon? She was not only putting herself in danger, but possibly those around her, too. Simon had already proven he would stop at nothing – including murder – to get what he wanted: *her*.

The truth was, she didn't belong in Birch Falls any more than she did anywhere else, and she couldn't afford any more ties. Between looking out for herself and trying to keep her sisters safe, she had enough to handle.

The ride was far too short. Once again, Bailey was reluctant to release her hold on her warm, dark knight, but this time it had nothing to do with fear. She removed herself from the bike with care, pulling down her skirt modestly. Michael got off the bike, too.

"How can I thank you?" she asked, fully aware

that it was a loaded question.

Michael gave her a roguish smile and took her hand in his. He bent forward, skimming the tips of her knuckles with his lips, his eyes never leaving her face. "Why, my lady, I believe you have already offered to feed me. Don't tell me you've changed your mind?"

"No. The offer stands."

Michael released her hand. She took several steps forward then looked back over her shoulder when she realized he wasn't following.

"You're not coming?"

"I have some things to take care of, but I'll be back."

"What things?" she asked, though she suspected she already knew. He didn't reply, but she could read the answer in his eyes clearly enough. "Michael, I appreciate the effort, but it's over."

"Hey, stop worrying, okay? I'll be back soon."

When he looked at her like that, eyes softened and slightly crinkled at the corners, full male lips curved in the hint of a reassuring smile, it was hard to do anything but believe him.

She nodded. "Guess I better start those rolls then."

"And coffee."

"And coffee," she agreed.

Bailey was two steps inside the door when she heard the deep rumble of his motorcycle roaring to life. She watched through the windows as he sped off into the night, already missing him and that sense of safety he unknowingly provided.

* * *

Michael

The sooner he took care of this, the sooner he'd be back with Bailey. That was the thought that propelled Michael through the back streets of Birch Falls at a speed well above the posted limit.

The woman twisted him inside out like nothing else. He prided himself on his self-control and his ability to withstand anything the enemy could throw at him. He was the fucking epitome of grace under pressure—except when Bailey Keehan was within one hundred yards. Then he had trouble remembering his own name. Something about her kicked him right into the red zone, no passing "GO," no collecting two hundred dollars.

Michael wondered vaguely if his grandfather had foreseen this happening, and that was why he'd been so adamant about his help as opposed to that of his Uncle Jack and his cousins in Pine Ridge. They specialized in ferreting out information and, ever so quietly, solving problems. Sure, he was no slouch when it came to covert ops, but the fact that Conlan had specifically chosen him instead of making that phone call was telling. Fortunate, too, because the thought of any of his single male cousins sniffing around Bailey was unacceptable.

Not that it mattered, really. If Bailey Keehan was his *croie* – and Michael was certain she was – then fate would have crossed their paths eventually. Conlan O'Leary might have had an ulterior motive when he provided the initial introduction, but the result would have been the same whether he'd met her at a gas station or the grocery store. There was no logical explanation for it; it just *was*.

The same thing had happened to his sister. His brother. His parents and grandparents. At a couple of years past the thirty mark, he'd accepted that it wasn't going to happen for him.

Sometimes, it was nice to be proven wrong.

chapter four

Michael

When Michael returned to Tommy's, he strode into the private back room with a definite purpose and a good deal of pent-up energy. He was pleased to see the guy from earlier sitting between Kyle and Johnny, looking rather unhappy. He wasn't a small man, yet he was dwarfed between the two of them.

The cocky look he'd worn earlier was gone now; his eyes flicked nervously around him, his body stiff with tension. Michael dropped into the chair opposite him, somewhat surprised that the guy wasn't pissing his pants yet. That was going to change.

Kyle tossed a wallet his way, earning a glower from the man. Michael opened it and rifled through the contents. Driver's license. Two hundred bucks, give or take. A MAC/debit card for the local bank. No credit cards, no photos, nothing personal. Michael kept his expression neutral, but inside, his gut wasn't just humming, it was rumbling like his Harley.

"Robert White," he mused, sliding the wallet back across the table. "Mind if I call you Rob?"

"What the hell do you want?"

Michael signaled for a server. One promptly appeared with a fresh longneck. When she walked away, Michael twisted the cap off and sat back. "Tell me about the girl."

Rob shrugged. "A misunderstanding, that's all."

"A misunderstanding, huh?"

"Yeah." Rob shifted. "I mean, you saw her. A hot chick like that, all alone in the bar, I thought I'd give it a shot."

"And she said no."

"I thought she was playing hard to get," Rob explained, glancing around the table for support, finding none.

"Hmmm," Michael hummed. "Have you been following her?"

Rob's expression changed from disgruntled to disbelief. It would have been convincing, too, if Michael hadn't seen the truth in the guy's eyes before he shielded it.

"Is that what she said? That I've been following her?"

Michael shrugged noncommittally. "Have you?"

"It's a small fucking town. We're bound to run

into each other once in a while. It doesn't mean anything."

"And a man can't help but notice someone like her. Pretty. Kind of fresh. Almost...innocent." Michael kept his tone casual. Interested.

"Yeah, exactly. So maybe I put in a little prep time, better my odds. That's not a crime."

Prep time. As in learning schedules, habits, social contacts. Not unlike what he had been doing at his grandfather's request. But what Michael had done was for an honorable purpose, whereas he didn't think Rob's was.

Unfortunately, though, Rob was right. Stalking wasn't a crime, not unless he threatened or caused physical harm or damage, which, as far as Michael knew, he hadn't. Which also meant that any action taken in this case would be of the non-official variety.

The guy didn't appear to have anything openly incriminating on him, but his plan had included getting Bailey out of the bar. The question was, then what?

Michael looked at Johnny. "Got his keys?"

"What the hell do you need my keys for?"

They ignored him. "Yeah," Johnny confirmed. "It's a rental. Silver KIA."

Michael laughed; he couldn't help it. This guy was too much. Nondescript appearance, nondescript name, nondescript car. But his body language gave him away. The way *Rob* (no way that was his real name) held himself – straight backed, arms slightly away from the body, unflinching – screamed former military.

"Nice story. Now tell me who you really are and what you want with her."

"Give me my fucking keys and let me the hell out of here."

So much for doing things the easy way. It didn't appear as if Rob was going to be cooperative.

"You're not ready to leave yet, are you, Rob? We're having such a nice chat." Michael's eyes grew cold and he leaned forward and lowered his voice. "And you still haven't answered my questions."

"Fuck you."

Michael's lips curled into a feral grin. "No, Rob. Fuck *you*."

"You won't do anything," Rob sneered. "Too many witnesses."

Michael gave him a smile that didn't quite reach his eyes. He stood up, looked around the room, and cleared his throat. Instantly, he had everyone's undivided attention.

"Oi! This piece of shit has been stalking that fine, young, Irish lady you all saw in here earlier. And not just *any* fine young Irish lady. *My* fine, young, Irish lady." Assorted gasps were heard throughout the room, Johnny's included. Michael waited, daring anyone to challenge him. No one did.

"He thinks that he will not be held accountable

for his actions because there are witnesses present. Does anyone here agree with him?"

There were a few seconds of dead silence. Only the pulsing beat from the main dance floor could be heard, the sound muffled by the thick cinderblock walls separating the back room from the public areas. Then a voice spoke up.

"What piece of shit would that be, Mike?" someone called from the other side of the room. "All I see here are a bunch of good ol' boys kicking back a few and shooting some pool."

Others murmured their agreement. Michael turned back to the table, holding up his hands and baring his teeth in the semblance of a smile. "Sorry, Rob."

Before Rob knew what hit him, Michael reached across the table and grabbed him by the collar. Johnny and Kyle moved back as Michael yanked Rob up from the chair, hauled him over the table then lifted him so that his toes hung a good inch from the floor.

Then he half-carried, half-dragged Rob to the back door.

Much to Rob's dismay, not one person seemed to have a problem with this. Several, in fact, seemed quite anxious to assist Michael in providing the lesson.

"Did that just actually *happen*?" Kyle asked, looking at Johnny in astonishment as they followed. Michael had just publicly declared he was claiming

Bailey as his woman. Word would spread like wildfire, and no one would dare make a move on her now. Unless she took up with Michael, she would be as untouchable as a cloistered nun.

Johnny seemed similarly stunned, but then a huge grin spread across his face. "I guess we know who the woman on his mind is now, huh? Wonder if she knows yet…"

* * *

Bailey

The clock struck one in the near-empty diner, and Michael still hadn't returned. Had he changed his mind?

Bailey looked worriedly out the window when she heard the sirens and saw an ambulance heading in the direction of Tommy's. Her thoughts turned darker. Had something happened? Had he been in an accident?

She breathed a sigh of relief a few minutes later, when Michael walked through the door looking as gorgeous as always and none the worse for wear. In fact, he looked even sexier than usual. He radiated power and purpose, his eyes bright and his hair windblown from the ride.

Exhilaration coursed through her. He had come back to see her, just as he said he would.

"Michael! You made it."

"I told you I would. You didn't doubt me, did you?"

She hesitated before answering, leading him to his favorite corner booth. Along the way, she picked up a freshly-made pot of coffee and the plate of rolls from the warmer.

"I heard the sirens. I thought maybe…" Bailey let the sentence hang, unwilling to give voice to her thoughts.

"You were worried about me, weren't you?" he asked, his lips twitching across the table. Bailey slid in across from him, grateful for the late night lull in business.

He savored each bite of the gooey roll as if it was the best dessert he'd ever had. A tiny glob of icing stuck to his slightly fuller bottom lip. She couldn't help her sharp intake of breath when his tongue peeked out and cleared it away. Parts of her body lit up and tingled as she imagined him licking *her* like that.

Embarrassed by the direction her thoughts had taken, her cheeks pinked a rosy hue and her eyes dropped shyly. "It's silly, I know," she said, finding the way her fingers folded and unfolded in her lap suddenly very interesting. "I'm sure you are more than capable of taking care of yourself. I mean, you're so…"

Once again, Bailey didn't finish her sentence, feeling foolish. Surely, he was well acquainted with his own large, capable body. Just the little bit she'd felt earlier promised her endless nights of hot, steamy dreams. In any event, he certainly didn't need her to tell him. He probably had women falling over him all the time.

She could picture it so clearly. A veritable harem of females crowding around him, hoping to be the one he chose. *Oh Michael, you're so big and strong.* The corners of her mouth curved upward. Then other phrases popped unbidden into her mind. *Oh Michael, what big muscles you have. Oh Michael, what a big..."*

A rush of heat flooded her and her cheeks burned when she recalled the way he'd pulled her against him earlier at Tommy's. Specifically, that large, thick evidence of desire that had pressed into her belly.

Oh Michael, indeed.

He was watching her closely, which only exacerbated her embarrassment.

"So...what?" he prompted.

Oh, no. She wasn't going there. She sipped her coffee, moistening her suddenly dry throat and took a different path.

"Tell me, do you make a habit of coming to the aid of damsels in distress, Michael?"

He grinned, sending her heartbeat into an erratic pattern. "Only the ones who kiss like you do."

"I'm..." She wanted to say she was sorry about what had happened, but that would be a bald-faced lie. That kiss made her feel a lot of things, but regret wasn't one of them. So instead, she lowered her head and studied her hands some more.

He reached across the table to place his finger under her chin, lifted it so that she would look at him.

"Not to put too fine a point on it, but you had everyone at Tommy's so hot for you tonight that I felt compelled to lay claim."

Her head snapped up. "You did *what*?"

"I called dibs." He gave her a boyish grin that made her insides clench, then soften into something gooey. "To protect your honor, of course. They're a wild bunch, to be sure, and I cannot permit any suggestion of impropriety."

Bailey's lips quirked. "Do you take it upon yourself to safeguard the honor of maidens often?"

He looked at her intently, his green eyes glowing. "Since I have not come across many *maidens*, I would have to say no. You're the first."

He was teasing, she knew, by throwing her own word back at her, but it was the truth. By her reckoning, she was one of the last among a dying breed of twenty-five-year-old virgins. It wasn't that she hadn't wanted to, or that she wasn't curious. She did and she was. But she wanted it to *mean* something beyond experience points or satisfying her curiosity. Since she avoided relationships and couldn't allow herself to get close to anyone, anything more than a one-night stand was next to impossible.

Michael was a bit of an exception, though. Despite her best efforts to remain distant, he'd managed to burrow under her armor with his quiet intensity and repeated visits. And then there was the whole knight fantasy. If only her problems could be solved with him riding in on his white horse and slaying her dragons.

"Why does my honor concern you so?"

"Because I'm going to marry you." Michael's mouth curved up into an angelic smile that robbed her of her breath momentarily.

Her insides twisted and clenched again, even though she knew he was only kidding. She swallowed through the pain to play along. "Don't I get a say in this?"

"Of course. You get to say 'yes' and 'I do'."

Bailey laughed and it felt good. There was something about him that left her feeling off-kilter, but in a good way. She liked that she didn't know what he would say or do next. Michael's unpredictability was fun and exciting, not frightening or threatening.

chapter five

Michael

Michael shrugged. He could tell she had no idea he was telling her the honest truth. He *was* going to marry her; that was a given. He'd decided that about a minute or so after he'd realized who and what she was to him, but clearly, she hadn't reached the same conclusion yet.

And while she *was* coming around, they had a long way to go.

He finished off the last of his roll, then wiped his mouth with a napkin, taking personal satisfaction in the way her eyes lingered on his lips. "You may feel free to use your baking skills to seduce me at any time."

Bailey smiled and he felt the incredible power of it course through his veins. *Some veins more than others*, he thought, as he shifted slightly beneath the table.

"Is that all it takes to win your attention?" she

teased. "A cinnamon roll and a cup of coffee?"

"That was the best cinnamon roll I have *ever* had. And this is really good coffee." She laughed, the sound like music to his ears. "But it's not enough, I'm afraid."

Such a cute pout, too. "Oh? I thought we had a deal."

"We did. But you did get to ride my trusty steed, and I neglected to factor that in. That costs extra, you see."

"Indeed," she mused thoughtfully. "So, I'm still in your debt then, am I?"

"I'm afraid so."

"Hmmm. Will it be another roll?" Michael grinned and shook his head.

"More coffee?"

"Nope."

"Then what?"

His grin widened. "A kiss."

* * *

Bailey

"A kiss?" Bailey caught her breath, instantly recalling the mind-numbing lip-locker he'd given her earlier. Granted, she had been the one to initiate it, but he'd gone above and beyond. *She* should be paying *him* for another one of those.

"Aye." He winked.

"What kind of kiss, exactly?"

"I will leave that up to you, my lady. You may decide what you think is a fair price to pay for my knightly services."

"You mean I could give you a peck on the cheek and you would consider that payment in full?"

"If you feel that's all I am worth, certainly."

Oh, he was good. "And when is this payment due?"

"That is also entirely up to you."

She appeared to give this some serious thought, but in her mind, there was no question she would be kissing this man again.

"What happens if I don't settle our account right away?"

"I will keep returning until you do." His lips quirked.

That sounded awesome, *if* she was going to be around. Which she wasn't, she reminded herself. Now, more than ever – before things became even more complicated. Before any more "stalkers" showed up.

Before she fell any harder for Michael Connelly.

"And if I choose to kiss you right now?"

Michael placed his hand over his heart. "Then your debt will be paid in full. Though I fear, my lady, I shall be returning evermore."

The words flowed from his lips, smooth and

sweet as honey. Men had come onto her before, but none had ever reached deep inside and wrapped around her heart as he had. In that moment, she could think of nothing she wanted more.

"I think I would like to kiss you now."

"As you wish."

Bailey made up her mind before she lost her nerve. There was no way she was going to let such an opportunity slip by. She licked her lips, slid out of the booth, and … came face to chest with the owner.

"Oh! Mr. O'Leary, I'm sorry, I didn't see you there."

The older man smiled at her, then at Michael with a knowing look. Of course, he knew. She could feel the guilt and embarrassment coloring her cheeks; he'd probably heard every word.

Bailey smoothed down her uniform and suddenly realized that she'd spent the last thirty minutes sitting in a booth with Michael when she was supposed to be working.

"I'll just get back to work then," she stammered. "I'll stay past my shift, of course, to make up for this."

Conlan patted her shoulder soothingly. "You'll do nothing of the sort. What could I possibly need you to do, lass? Business is slow tonight. You've already cleaned every table, refilled the shakers, and done enough baking to carry me through the next few days."

That was true enough. She'd been doing her best to keep occupied while waiting (hoping) for Michael's return and she may have been slightly overzealous.

His eyes twinkled mischievously. "I was coming out to tell you to leave early tonight."

"Really?"

"Aye. You've earned a night off, I'm thinking. Only thing is, I can't leave till Meg comes in at seven, and I can't see you walking home alone in the middle of the night…"

His eyes flicked toward Michael, who immediately got to his feet. "I'd be happy to see her home safely."

"Aye," the old man chuckled. "Somehow I thought you might. Is that all right with you, lass?"

All right? It was more than all right. Anticipation welled up inside her at the thought of having a few extra stolen moments with Michael. "Yes."

"Then it's settled. Go on now, get your things."

* * *

Michael

When Bailey disappeared into the back, Conlan's smile faded and he regarded Michael seriously. "I know I asked you to do this as a special favor, but I saw the way the lass was looking at you. It's gone beyond that now, hasn't it?"

"Yes."

"You might be my grandson, but I'm telling you right now – if you hurt that lass, I'm going to take it out of your arse, do you hear me?"

Michael grinned. "*Daideo*, that woman is going to be my bride. She's going to give you an entire brood of great-grandchildren. She just doesn't know it yet."

The old man slapped Michael on the back and let out a hearty bark of laughter. "That's my boy."

* * *

Bailey

When Bailey returned a few minutes later, she had the distinct impression she'd missed something. Both men were laughing and smiling. She looked from one to the other. When they stood next to one another like that, she could see a definite resemblance. They shared the same overall build, angled, masculine features, and slightly crooked grins.

Then Michael's luminous green gaze turned her way and her mind went blank.

"Your trusty steed awaits, my lady," Michael said with a slight bow, making her giggle. The way he looked at her made her forget nearly everything else, except the promise of the kiss she "owed" him. Placing her hand in his, feeling his long fingers closing around hers as his warmth seeped into her, she could think of little else.

"Why do you work nights?" Michael asked her as they walked hand in hand out to the parking lot.

She shrugged, offering a partial truth. There was no way she was going to tell him that nighttime was when most bad things happened, when vigilance was key. Daytime was far safer, when there were fewer shadows and more eyes watching.

"My inner clock's nocturnal, I guess."

He seemed to accept that. "Have you ever seen the sun rise over the lake?"

"No, I can't say that I have." She'd watched the dawn arrive often enough, but her view was usually limited to brief glimpses through the huge panes of diner glass during the early morning rush.

"Would you like to?"

Watching a sunrise over the lake with Michael Connelly was definitely something she'd like to do. The question was, should she?

The short answer was no, she shouldn't. Every minute she spent with him now was only going to make it harder to leave later, and she did have to leave. Simon might already know where she was. Staying in Birch Falls would only bring him here, and that was the last thing she wanted. This was a nice place, with nice people who didn't deserve that kind of trouble.

No, as much as she might wish otherwise, she could not have a relationship with Michael.

But you could have this moment, right now, a little voice murmured in the back of her mind. And really, that's all anyone had, wasn't it?

"With you? Yes, I would. Very much."

His resulting smile had an instant liquefying effect on her insides. No one had ever been able to melt her with just a look before, which only reinforced her decision. To stay a few steps ahead of Simon, she needed her insides solid and intact.

"How about I take you back to your place so you can get changed first? Don't get me wrong, I think that little waitress uniform is sexy as hell, but riding up to the lake and back in that skirt won't be comfortable for you."

Bailey forgot to breathe for a few seconds. He thought she looked sexy? Self-conscious, she smoothed down the front and sides of her skirt.

He grinned wolfishly. "Too late, my lady. The damage is already done."

Feeling very feminine, she took her place on the back of his bike, savoring the chance to wrap her arms around him. Once again, the ride was too short. She'd barely had a chance to indulge in a single fantasy about what it would be like to straddle him while he was on the bike before he was pulling up in front of the building.

"Would you like to come in?" she asked, unsure exactly what the protocol was.

"I think I'll just wait out here, if you don't mind." He leaned against the cycle, casually crossing one ankle over the other. He looked so hot, so supremely male, it took her breath away. Until she realized he'd rejected her offer. Had she completely misread the situation?

"You don't want to come in?"

His blazing eyes sent a wave of reassuring heat through her. One side of his mouth tilted up in a grin as he slowly shook his head from side to side. "I promised I'd take you to see the sunrise over the lake."

"Oh."

"And if I stepped foot into your apartment, I doubt we'd be making it out anytime soon."

For just a moment, the ground seemed to sway beneath her feet, and the word "swoon" popped into her mind. She inhaled sharply, drawing in much-needed oxygen to clear away the lusty fog that wrapped around her.

"Why is that?" she asked breathlessly.

"My lady," he said with a tilt of his head, "I may be a knight, but I am *not* a saint."

* * *

Michael

Bailey's eyes widened slightly then softened, gifting him with a radiant smile. Then she cupped his face in her hands, threaded her fingers into his hair, and kissed him fully on the lips. Her tongue reached out and skimmed along his bottom lip, a silent request. He opened for her, groaning at the feel of her tongue sweeping along his.

Once again, she had surprised him by taking the lead. And once again, he was totally on board with that. He snaked his arms around her waist and pulled her closer, deepening the kiss. He could get lost in her, feeling the connection far beyond his lips. Heat swirled through him, flooding his veins with warmth that came not from her hot little body, but from somewhere much, much deeper.

He'd never experienced anything like it.

As much as he would have liked to explore those sensations more thoroughly, the sound of an approaching car and the sweep of oncoming headlights reminded him where they were. He broke the kiss reluctantly. Bailey remained close up against him, face lifted, eyes closed, lips parted and red.

"I take it your accounts are now paid in full?" he asked, his voice husky.

Those long, dark lashes rose slowly, right along with the devilish smile curling those ravished lips. "Not even close," she murmured. "*That* was just a down payment."

He groaned, because *damn*, and forced his hands to let go. "Go on with you, then. I'll wait here."

She nodded, looking as if she didn't want to leave him any more than he wanted her to. It was almost enough for him to say the hell with it and save the sunrise for another day. The woman was temptation personified, stretching him to the limits of his self-control. Didn't she have any idea how close he was to the breaking point? This raw, clawing need continued to grow (another sign that she was his *croie*), and was now to the point where it was downright scary.

He reminded himself that he was going for the big payoff. Not just her body, but her heart and soul as well.

And nothing less than forever would do.

When Bailey came out a few minutes later, Michael was glad he was still leaning against the bike, because his knees went positively weak. Heeled boots in black leather, body-hugging low-riding black jeans, a silky black camisole that gave teasing little flashes of a gold chain with some sort of charm around her navel, and a turquoise chamois shirt, left unbuttoned and hanging open.

In her right hand she carried a jacket of soft, black leather that she slid on as she walked, and a canvas backpack. Then she gathered her hair behind her, the motion fluid and practiced, to fasten it in a clip, allowing strands to fall loosely around her face. Michael caught additional flashes of fine gold chains in her ears, and knew they would match the one he'd glimpsed near her navel.

Sweet Mary, Mother of God. He swallowed hard, questioning the sanity of being anywhere alone with this woman looking like *that*. His heart thumped forcefully; his hands itched with the need to touch.

"Is this okay?" she asked as she approached the bike.

Michael nodded. He didn't trust himself to speak.

* * *

Bailey

"Are you sure?" Bailey bit her lip and shifted nervously from one foot to the other, growing increasingly anxious by the second. Other than the tiny nod, Michael hadn't moved an inch since she'd come out. It was as if he was frozen, turned to stone. Only his eyes moved, following her forward progress.

He blinked. Once.

"I'll go change," she said quickly, turning to run back into the building. She'd picked out the outfit carefully, shooting for something casual and practical, but sexy, too. Obviously, she'd chosen poorly.

She'd barely taken two steps before Michael was behind her, turning her and pulling her into his arms and devouring her with his lips. His hands moved down her back and over her backside, pressing her closer against him. Once again, she felt his solid steel shaft on her belly. Unlike his previous kisses, which were powerful but well-controlled, this one was wild, desperate.

And exactly what her flailing confidence needed.

* * *

Michael

"Don't change." His voice was thick and raspy, his words spoken with great effort. He rested his forehead against hers, and forced his hands up to the small of her back, while he tried to catch his breath. He was doing his best to move slowly with her, not an easy thing when his body was conspiring against him.

"I'm sorry," he whispered. Bailey's hands reached up and cupped his face, a moment before she pressed her lips to his. Michael groaned and swept his tongue against hers, drinking in her sweetness as if his life depended on it. Given the way his heart was pounding, it just might.

"You look perfect, just the way you are."

Her eyes opened slowly, her gaze unfixed and distant, and he thought it was the sexiest look in the world. At least until her eyes focused on his and filled with flames of pure desire. Yep, definitely sexier. His cock throbbed painfully against her warmth. It took every ounce of self-control he possessed to not toss her over his shoulder, carry her into her apartment, and claim her right then and there.

"Come on," he said huskily, lacing his fingers briefly through hers. Even that simple connection with her felt amazingly intimate. "I promised you a sunrise."

"Aye," she whispered softly. "That you did."

Those few words, spoken with the perfect lilt of an Irish maiden, were nearly his undoing. Michael hadn't realized until that moment how much his heritage meant to him, or how deeply ingrained it was.

"Ah, lass, you doona wan' ta be goin' there," he whispered against her ear, "'cause you wouldna be seein' the sunrise anytime soon."

Michael felt the full-body shiver that rippled through her, welcoming it with an internal shiver of his own. With great reluctance, he managed to release her, then mounted his bike with particular care. She glided gently behind him, wrapping herself around him like a second skin. Without another word, they rode away.

chapter six

Michael

It was amazing how quickly Bailey had taken to riding on the back of a motorcycle. She was a natural, with an excellent sense of balance. She became adept at recognizing even the slightest nuances in Michael's movements, adjusting without conscious thought.

The ride was more difficult for Michael. Feeling her hands around his waist, her body pressed tightly against his for a prolonged period of time, was torture, but it was a torture he gladly endured. Being with his *croie* was a novel experience; it would take some time to adjust to the powerful urges clawing not only at his body, but his heart and mind as well.

It was still dark when they arrived at the lake. The sky was an incredible shade of velvety midnight blue with a myriad of stars reflecting upon the still water along with the final traces of a waning crescent moon. Michael parked the bike in the small gravel lot and led her up a slight incline to a scenic spot overlooking the eastern shore.

"There," he said, indicating the large, flat rock ledge a short distance away. "Best seat in the house for a sunrise, guaranteed." He helped her up onto the rock, getting a delicious view of her ass in the process, before climbing up himself. He withheld his groan, but just barely. She wasn't making this any easier by being so damn desirable.

Bailey produced a small blanket from the pack she'd brought along and proceeded to spread it out. Michael raised an eyebrow, glad for the distraction, however slight.

"Seemed like a good idea," she said with a shrug of her shoulders.

"It was," he agreed. He lowered himself onto it, leaning back against the incline, wishing he'd thought of it himself. Normally he was well-prepared for a mission, but organized, practical thoughts seemed to fly out the window when it came to her.

Michael patted the space in front of him in invitation. Bailey eased herself between his thighs, resting her back against his chest. "Is this okay?" she asked over her shoulder.

"Perfect." His arms slid beneath hers so that his hands rested comfortably on her belly. She snuggled into him a little more. Some of the fire in his blood settled with the contact, a soothing stroke to his ragged need. If he couldn't be inside her, then having her soft, fragrant weight pressing against him was the next best thing.

"Are you cold?"

"No," she answered. "You're very warm."

Honey, I'm going to burst into flames if I get any warmer.

Her temple rested against his jaw; her silken waves teased his neck. He couldn't help himself; he turned slightly and pressed his lips to her soft, supple skin.

"Mm. That's nice," she murmured.

Yeah, it was. And since he didn't want it to end any time soon, he forced himself to behave.

They sat like that for a while, enjoying the quiet serenity. It was a beautiful spot off the beaten path, one known only to a few. He, Johnny, and Lina had discovered it when they were kids, having spent most of their summers at the family's cabin nearby.

Just down below and to the right was one of his father's favorite fishing spots. And to the left, the evergreen-laden shore jutted out in a slight curve, hiding them from the nearby public boat launch.

With her body tucked close and his arms resting lightly over her waist, Michael closed his eyes and breathed in her scent. For as jacked up as he was, he felt oddly at peace, too. That restlessness that had been nagging him as of late—for most of his life, really—was noticeably absent.

He wondered again at the mysterious, formidable power of *croies*.

"So..." she finally said, "did you take care of whatever you had to do tonight?"

Her voice was casual, but he heard the undercurrent beneath the words. He'd hoped she wouldn't ask, but he wasn't surprised that she had, either.

"Yes."

"Did it have anything to do with the guy that was harassing me?"

Should he tell her the truth? That, after finding the hypodermic needles, sedatives, ropes, and rolls of duct tape in the guy's car, he'd beaten the son-of-a-bitch to within an inch of his life? Should he tell her that imagining what Rob might have done to her if he'd gotten her out of Tommy's made him lose his shit? That the only reason he wasn't facing murder charges was because Kyle and Johnny had pulled him off the guy at the last minute?

He wanted her to feel safe. To know that as long as he was around, she never had to be afraid again. At the same time, he was concerned that the lengths to which he was willing to go to ensure her safety might be more than she could handle at this early stage of their relationship. Just because he'd come to the realization that she was his future didn't mean that she had.

Yeah, he was intense. Yeah, he had the knowledge and skills to do some damage. And yeah, he protected what was his (which now included her). On some level, she probably already sensed that or she wouldn't have run into his arms. She'd learn about the rest soon enough. But, since her trust was still new and fragile, he'd keep the detailed disclosures to a minimum.

"Does the name Robert White mean anything to you?"

She thought about it for a moment, then shook her head. "No. Is that his name?"

He nodded, though he was pretty sure it was an alias. "What do you know about him?"

Her body shifted. Beneath his hands, he felt her stomach tighten, then release. "I already told you. I saw him around town a few times, and last night he came on to me at the bar."

"That's all?"

Another shift. "Yeah. Why?"

Not outright lies, but she wasn't telling him everything, either, which worried him. With the known threat eliminated, her fear should be, too, but his gut was telling him there was more.

"Because he had things in his car that suggested he had more in mind than a good time."

* * *

Bailey

Bailey felt the color drain from her face, glad

Michael was behind her and couldn't see it. "Like what?"

With her head resting against his jaw, she both heard and felt the grinding of his teeth.

"Tell me, Michael."

"Rope. Sedatives. Tape. Pictures of you. He's obsessed with you, Bailey. Based on his setup, I don't think you're the first woman he's targeted."

Icy dread slithered down the length of her spine, making her shiver. Her instincts had been right, telling her it was time to run. Either the guy was some kind of serial psycho, or he had been hired to abduct her and take her to Simon. She was betting on the latter, all but confirming her worst fears.

"It's okay," Michael said softly, holding her close. "He won't be bothering you, or anyone else for that matter, ever again."

She wanted to ask exactly how he knew that, then decided she didn't want to know.

"Thank you," she said softly.

"I won't let anything happen to you, Bailey."

That was the second time he'd said those words to her, and both times, she'd believed him. But the situation had changed, and he had no idea what he was up against.

She thought briefly of confiding in him, but dismissed the idea almost as quickly. Michael might be a strong, capable protector, but Simon was powerful, with nearly unlimited funds at his disposal, and a long reach.

Besides, for all of her romantic fantasies, Bailey was a practical person. Michael was being attentive, but she didn't believe for one minute that he was falling for her the same way she was for him.

Oh, she knew about Michael Connelly and his reputation with the ladies. It was hard not to when you lived in a small town like Birch Falls and worked in a place like O'Leary's. Everyone knew everyone else's business, and she'd heard a lot of it over the past six months. Michael Connelly's name had come up several times, a popular topic of conversation among the single female locals that appeared at the diner after the bars closed.

It was hard to reconcile the Michael they spoke of with the quiet, sweet man who showed up every Friday night for coffee. He was every bit as drop-dead gorgeous as she'd heard, but had none of the full-on ego of the lady killer she'd expected. Instead he had an almost shy, boyish smile, and when he spoke, it was with a low, musical cadence. In all the times she'd seen him, he'd been nothing but a perfect gentleman.

And the way he held her, as if she was truly special to him, was playing havoc with her reason.

Part of her had begun to wonder if those rumors hadn't been more wishful thinking than anything else. After all, she'd entertained some pretty explicit fantasies about him herself.

And, while she was seriously considering making some of those fantasies a reality very, very soon, she could not allow her heart to be broken in the process. She could have this morning. Then it was time to move on, before anyone found out the truth.

Before she lost any more of her heart to him.

* * *

Michael

Off in the distance, the sky began to lighten into the softest pastel shades of blue, green and yellow. Michael couldn't remember when holding a woman felt so good. Probably never, since he'd never had a woman he'd wanted to simply hold in his arms.

Then again, he'd never been with his *croie* before. Even sitting there, the rhythmic beat of their hearts the only communication, he could feel his soul beginning to knit with hers.

"Do you come up here often?" she asked, tracing small figure eights on the back of his hand. She sounded relaxed, content. Very little, if any, of her usual wariness was present, which was amazing, considering what he'd just told her.

It was another step forward. Michael wanted her to feel safe with him, to trust him.

"No, not really. My family used to come up

here when I was a kid."

"It's so beautiful."

"Yes," he agreed. "You are." He felt, rather than saw, her smile. There was no mistaking the feel of her body melting into his, radiating warm heat. Beneath the denim, his cock pulsed with ache in perfect time to his heart.

Stop it, he silently commanded.

"Michael?"

"Hmmm?"

"This is really nice. Thanks for bringing me here."

"You're welcome." He pressed his lips to her cheek again. "But next time, I'm going to remember to bring some of your incredible coffee and cinnamon rolls."

"Oh, I almost forgot." She sat up and reached for her backpack. Before he could protest her absence, she pulled out a stainless steel Thermos and a small package wrapped in aluminum foil. He gazed in wonder as she poured him a cup of her special blend and unwrapped a roll for him. "Here, it's still warm."

"You cannot possibly be real," he said, taking a sip and closing his eyes in sheer pleasure. "You are a genuine angel." Bailey laughed softly. Even in the predawn light, he could see the rosy tint rising in her cheeks.

"Come on, you can tell me. I'll keep your secret." He winked.

"Hardly," she laughed. "But I'm glad you think so."

"My lady, there is no doubt in my mind that you were sent from heaven for me and me alone. What I can't figure out is, what I did to deserve you." He gave her a mischievous smile. "I'm just not that good."

"I think you're wonderful," she breathed.

Something shifted deep inside him. He set the coffee down, the need to kiss her a tangible thing. He needed it more than he needed to breathe.

"Bailey?"

"Yes?"

"I think I'd like the rest of that payment now."

Bailey twisted around and straddled his thighs, resting her palms on his shoulders. Michael's hands held her hips, pulling her towards him. For as long as he lived, he would never forget how she looked in that moment. A beautiful angel, framed by golden light as the sun broke over the horizon.

"The sun is rising," he murmured as her hands cupped his face and she lowered her head to his.

"I know," she whispered, her lips brushing against his. "A kiss at sunrise is the most magical of all."

That was the last thing Michael heard before his world exploded. Bailey's lips met his, and he was lost. Her tongue was in his mouth, making the most wonderful strokes against his lips, against his tongue. She suckled and nipped gently, slanting her head to perfect the fit and bring them closer. Her fingers combed into his hair and flexed, the slight tug and scrape of her nails traveling like an electric current straight into his groin. His mind went into freefall while his heart soared to the heavens.

Then she tilted her pelvis and rocked against him, adding a few shooting stars to the mix.

"Bailey, stop," he breathed, stilling her movements with his big hands.

"Why?" Her lips moved over his jaw, over the pounding pulse in his neck. "You don't like it?"

"I like it too much," he admitted. "Much more and I won't be able to stop."

She pulled away just enough for him to see the hunger in her eyes. "You say that like it's a bad thing."

"Isn't it?"

"No."

Fisting his hair, she pulled him back to her as if she couldn't get enough. He captured her tiny, desperate moans in his mouth, making them his own.

She wants this. One word to the contrary and he'd force himself to stop, even if that meant taking an impromptu dip in the cold waters of the spring-fed lake. But if she was feeling this intense pull, too, the very rightness of it, then they didn't have to stop, they could begin their life together sooner rather than later.

"Bailey." He cupped her face and waited until

he had her full, undivided attention. "Baby, are you sure?"

She licked her lips. "Yes. I'm sure. I want this. I want you."

He'd fought the good fight but there was no use denying it any longer, not if it was what they both wanted.

Michael lost the capacity for rational thought as he gave himself over to it, surrendering the last of his control. His entire world was reduced to this one woman. She was the only thing that mattered.

His hand cupped the back of her head while he tasted her sweet mouth. Kissed the soft skin along her jaw and down her neck. Her body heat rose up from under that sexy, silky camisole, and released a scent that nearly drove him insane.

Her scent. The scent of *his* woman.

He breathed deeply, allowing it to fill him with its intoxicating power. Never before had he felt the power of a woman so acutely. Even the slightest touch of her delicate hands was like a brand on his flesh, claiming and possessive.

He felt her breasts swell and her nipples harden beneath that tiny sheath of black silk, and his other hand was suddenly there, cupping her. A deeper moan escaped and it sent fire through his veins. His mouth dipped, suckling her through the silk as she arched into him.

"Oh, Michael," she moaned.

Hearing his name on her lips was like throwing

lighter fluid onto an already-raging fire. He wanted to hear her screaming it as he brought her to climax, over and over again. His hand reached under the cami to skim her searing flesh. She drew in a breath and whimpered, pressing into his palm.

"Sweet Jesus, Bailey, you're so fucking soft."

"And you're so fucking hard."

Her raw reply was accompanied by a lower body roll that brought those stars back into his vision, even brighter than before.

He gently kneaded her flesh, afraid that his roughened hands would hurt her. Lifting her top, he paused to look at her perfect, round breasts – so full and begging to be sucked.

"You are perfection." *His* perfection. To finally be able to touch and taste her like this was sheer bliss. He dipped his head and laved each one, taking each nipple alternately into his mouth and rolling it over his tongue.

Bailey's chest heaved, greedy for more as her nails dug into his scalp. With some effort, he slid the button-down over her shoulders and lifted the cami over her head. In the span of a heartbeat, her hands were back on him, coaxing and pleading for more. Short nails dug into his skin in a clawing demand.

Her hips ground into his erection in a wordless plea. Anxious to please, he wrapped one arm around her waist and rolled her beneath him. His mouth was on hers, then her neck as he kissed his way down to her navel. His fingers continued to play and pluck her now-stiff nipples while he licked around the fine gold charm with the emerald stone that dangled from her navel piercing.

So fucking sexy.

He'd never seen anything quite like it before – tiny, intertwined hearts topped by a crown embedded with a tiny emerald. A second golden charm lay beneath it. That one he knew – a Celtic cross. The whole piece was barely more than a half inch square, but it was exquisite.

"This is beautiful," he murmured against her skin, drawn to its intricate crafting.

"It's a *luckenbooth*," she said, breathless. "Scottish."

"I thought you were an Irish lass," he teased, nipping at her hips. He saw the same crown symbols there, tattooed on the inside of her left hip.

"Scottish dad, Irish mom," she panted.

"So where is your Irish heritage represented?" he asked, his words muffled against her flesh as he kissed his way across her abdomen. Impatient hands unfastened her jeans and tugged them down past her hips, stoked to find that she was every bit aroused as he was. He breathed deeply, hardwiring the sight and scent of her arousal into his primitive control center.

"Left shoulder blade. Celtic cross."

Michael vowed to verify that later, but his view at the moment was just too compelling to break away.

Unable to wait another moment, he lowered his head and nuzzled against her sex. She gasped and arched upward as his hands parted her thighs to delve deeper. Nestling his lips between her silky flesh, he growled his approval.

Pleasing her became his only purpose. Everything up to this point had been merely preparation for this. For her.

His hands moved of their own accord, caressing her soft, fragrant skin. Grasped her hips. Pulled her closer to better continue his feast.

Michael licked her folds with long, slow, savoring strokes while she tangled her hands in his hair and begged him for more. Each cry of strangled pleasure brought forth another surge of desire to take her even farther. He wanted more, needed more of her sweet, creamy confection in his mouth, on his face. He thrust his tongue deep into her entrance, growing drunk on her essence.

She rocked her hips against his face, her movements faster, her tugs more insistent, and he knew she was close. Replacing his tongue with his fingers, he flat-tongued it back up to her sensitive nub and sucked hard.

"Michael!"

Her scream rent through the still morning air; her thighs locked around his head as a series of tremors rolled through her.

Triumph exploded in his chest. *So responsive.*

So fucking mine.

Michael kissed her through the after-shocks. Only when her thighs started shaking did she begin to relax her hold.

"Oh my God, Michael," she breathed. "That was amazing."

Hell yes, it was.

He could remain buried between her legs for hours, bringing her to climax again and again. She was like a drug and he had just become her biggest junkie, already jonesing for another fix. He returned to gentle licks and soothing suckles at her tender lips.

One finger eased inside her, sliding through her slick heat. It was a fortunate thing, too, because she was impossibly tight. One large finger stroked her from the inside while his thumb massaged her on the outside. He drew his mouth away just long enough to look at her. Her skin was flushed and glistening, smooth and bare and beautiful.

And *his*. As he was now hers.

He knew that as surely as he knew his own name. Better, because he couldn't actually recall his own name at that moment. All he knew for sure was that he was hers, just as she was his. His *croie*, his everything.

Her body protested his absence and he felt the pads of her fingers against his scalp again as her contented mews began to grow needy again. Her desperate little moans were music to his ears.

"Michael, *please*."

He loved hearing her beg for relief, loved hearing his name coming from her mouth as she cried out for him. He would oblige. He would pleasure her as no man ever had. By the time he was through, she would have forgotten every other man she had ever known. From this day forward, she would only know him. He swore it to God under his breath, seared the oath into his soul. In claiming her, he had surrendered himself, a silent vow to devote the rest of his life to loving her as only he could.

"What do you want, Bailey?" he whispered against her sex, his breath sending convulsive shudders through her.

Her simple answer both thrilled and shattered him. "You."

Michael lifted himself up, placing his chest between her thighs and kissing her belly.

"What do you need, angel? This?" Two fingers slid into her again as he licked at her belly. She was drenched; the way she clenched around his fingers made his cock weep in envy. His balls ached so much he could barely stand it. She was doing things to him he couldn't control. He had to get inside her. *Now*. His cock strained, the pain almost unbearable.

He ripped open his shirt with one hand so he could feel her satiny skin against his own.

"Oh my God, yes! You feel so good, Michael."

He moved farther up her body, continuing to thrust his finger slowly inside her, making small, slow circles with his thumb on the outside to stoke the burn. All too soon, he felt her inner walls tightening again signaling her impending orgasm, and began to withdraw slowly. This time, he wanted to feel her come with him deep inside her. He needed it, craved it. Wanted the feel of her clenching around him, arching her body against him, screaming into his neck.

Her small hands dug into his shoulders; her legs wrapped around his hips. He chuckled against her skin, but it was a strangled sound. Liquid fire raced through his veins, consuming him from the inside out. There was no going back now. Not ever. To stop was to die in her arms.

His tongue licked the underside of her breast, distracting her while he shucked his pants. With his heavy cock resting against the silky skin of her inner thigh, she turned her hips, creating a cradle of bliss, arching her body into his as he took the tip of her breast into his mouth.

* * *

Bailey

"Michael!" she screamed, out of her mind with desire. She writhed beneath him, opening her legs wider, loving the heavy feel of his body weight as she cradled him. She tilted her hips, desperate to ease the sweet, excruciating ache that he'd built to another teetering crescendo.

This was what making love was supposed to be like – fiery passion, desperate need, wanting him more than she'd ever wanted anything. It was exactly what she'd been holding out for, and finally, she would have it.

It was a bittersweet moment, knowing that this would be a one-time deal. She didn't fool herself into thinking it was anything more than it was; a grand climax to the last eight weeks of fantasizing about him.

But it would be *spectacular*.

He held himself just above her, his elbows pressed closely against the sides of her breasts, his hands reaching up from behind and grasping her shoulders, the tip of his shaft poised where she needed him most. Perspiration slickened his chest, his breaths were ragged, his muscles corded and tense with the tremendous effort of holding back.

She felt his blunt head nudge against her, seeking her, parting her. He cradled her in his arms so tenderly, placing hot, wet kisses along her collarbone. Her writhing stopped, her hands ceased clawing, and she looked into his beautiful green eyes, awed by what she saw there.

So much hunger. So much passion. For her. Surely, he saw the same thing mirrored in hers.

But she should tell him. She should tell him now.

Michael returned her gaze and licked his lips.

"Bailey," he groaned, his voice breathless and thick with desire. Even his voice was making love to her. "Tell me to stop and I swear I will find a way."

Stop? No, she didn't want him to stop, but... *Tell him you're a virgin. Tell him you've never done this before and as much as you want him, you're scared, too.*

"I don't want you to stop, but—"

She didn't finish, because between one heartbeat and the next, her virginity was no more.

* * *

Michael

His last thread of control snapped as soon as the words crossed her lips. His mouth descended upon hers, capturing her cry as he rolled his hips and slid his cock deep in one swift, powerful stroke. Even with her wetness and his preparation, it was a tight fit.

And the best fucking thing he'd ever felt.

White noise buzzed in his head; his body shuddered with the ecstasy of being inside her. The bliss of it totally encompassed him, like sinking into a hot tub in the middle of a winter snowstorm. But even that analogy paled in comparison to the feel of what it was like to join with his *croie*.

For a moment he hung there as if in freefall,

simply losing himself in her. Then hot fire surged through his veins and the ache in his balls screamed at him to *move*.

Bailey screamed his name into his mouth and tensed beneath him as he felt her hot wetness burning against his shaft. She was so … fucking … tight. Her sheath clenched around him like a vise and he was forced to move slowly until she could stretch and accommodate his girth.

A thundering rumble replaced the white noise, filling his head, blocking out all else. The only thing remaining was a brutal, primal need to seal their bond, to find the heaven only she could provide. She was his. His to love. His to protect. His to please and pamper. No man would ever again know the searing heat of her skin or the soft yield of her flesh. He growled, a low menacing rumble that began deep in his chest and grew.

A tiny voice in the back of his head told him to go slowly, to give her time to adjust. She was right there with him, experiencing the intensity of their lovemaking, clinging to him as if her very life depended on it. There was time, plenty of time. The rest of their lives, in fact.

Another voice – the growling one – insisted that this could not wait. The need to mark her was too great and he was too desperate. She was so hot, so wet, so tight, and he *needed* her. After all those weeks of watching, of waiting, no other woman would do.

Especially when she'd begged so sweetly.

The scent of her - of her need - filled his nostrils; his mouth still held the taste of her sweet cream. Her slick body pressed against him from underneath, his hips seated between her open thighs, knees in the air... for him.

Her nails dug into his shoulders, scoring his skin. The sheer power of it overtook him and he thrust forward, burying himself to the hilt inside her. He felt her pushing against him, her natural resistance clenching around him, giving him the most incredible high. He heard her cries over the roaring in his head; he heard his name, but everything else was lost in his lusty haze.

Certain that he'd brought her to orgasm again, he could now allow his own. He answered by thrusting harder until his balls slammed against her, consumed by his desire to claim her. He was powerless against it, this raging need driving him over and over into her sweet flesh.

He nearly cried with relief when he felt his balls tighten and the seed rose in his shaft. With a final roar he crushed her to him and thrust deeply, riding wave after wave of ecstasy while he emptied inside her. Her body spasmed beneath his with each violent jet, prolonging his climax and making him come that much harder.

With his cock still buried deep and his face in her neck, he fell over her in convulsive shudders, attempting to recover from the most intense orgasm he'd ever experienced. That wasn't sex. It was a life-altering, mind-blowing, sharing of souls.

He had finally found the one he would spend the rest of his life with. The only one who could ever make him feel like this. As if he'd just injected his entire body into hers. As if his soul was now lodged somewhere deep in *her* chest, entwined forevermore with hers. She filled that part of him that had been missing, soothed the beast within him like no other. It was total bliss. Unfathomable utopia. He was home. He was whole. And he would never be the same again.

Returning to the confines of his physical body was harder than he thought. It was like trying to wake up and not being able to open your eyes, or trying to walk against the current in a raging, flooded stream. It was so much easier to just lie there in the wonderment of it all, letting things ease back slowly.

He didn't know how much time had actually passed before he realized her entire body was shaking beneath his, and he had his first inkling that something was wrong.

Bailey was too quiet. Except for the residual tremors, she wasn't moving. Tiny hitched breaths escaped from her throat. As his senses came back online, he realized he couldn't feel her hands on him anymore.

Michael lifted his head and the blood froze in his veins. Bailey's eyes were squeezed tightly shut, her face was drenched …. with tears? His heart stopped beating and his stomach filled with icy dread.

What had he done? Sweet Jesus, what had he just done?

chapter seven

Michael

"Bailey, sweetheart, what's wrong? Talk to me, baby."

A strangled sob bubbled out from her throat. Alarmed, he withdrew from between her legs – eliciting a cry of pain – and pushed himself to his knees. Her arms immediately came up and folded over her chest protectively.

"Shh, baby, don't cry, it's okay. I've got you." He pulled her to him, rocking her in his arms while his mind scrambled in blind panic.

Bailey's sobs against his chest felt like a blade cleaving him in two. "Did I hurt you? Oh, God, I did."

Michael cursed under his breath. It seemed the more he spoke, the harder she cried. Even more frightening was the way she curled herself into a ball, shutting herself away. He held her against him but her arms did not reach out for comfort; she drew them tightly against her body, hugging herself, retreating from him the only way she could.

He continued to rock her against him, not knowing what else to do. He held her in his lap, rubbing her back, stroking her hair while his heart ached.

Eventually her sobs quieted to little hiccups and he loosened his hold, though he continued the stroking. "Baby, I am so sorry," he whispered against the top of her head. Other than a sniffle or two, she remained silent.

Michael moved his hands to her shoulders. "Bailey, look at me, please." She kept her head down, shaking it ever so slightly. "*Please.*"

He placed his hand under her chin and tilted her face to him. Somehow, he managed to keep his voice gentle, nothing at all like the terror screaming inside of him. Slowly she raised her eyes to his and he stopped breathing altogether, because what he saw in those eyes nearly killed him. Hurt, pain, and… *shame.*

The look only lasted a second before she squeezed them shut again, pushing out a few more crystalline tears, but that look was burned into his brain forever. His hands dropped from her shoulders. That's when he noticed the blood – staining the blanket where she'd been laying, smeared across her lap and his. Not a lot, but enough to be visible in the stark light of early morning. His first thought was that she'd somehow been cut on the rocks, but the shocking truth hit him only a moment later with the force of a freight train.

"Sweet fucking Christ, Bailey. I didn't know! Why didn't you tell me?!"

The words came out with a harshness he hadn't intended, exploding out from the battle raging in his chest. She'd been a virgin, and he had just ravaged her. Pain shot through him like a white-hot poker when she flinched and turned away, but she couldn't hide the rise and fall of her shoulders that told him she was crying again.

Rage threatened to consume him – rage at himself for getting carried away like that, for not goddamned knowing, for not recognizing that impossible, tight resistance for what it had been.

The anger shifted, allowing an unfamiliar emotion to gain purchase: fear. Fear that by losing himself in the bliss that was his *croie*, he had hurt her.

So many things he should have done. He should have prepared her better, made sure she was ready for him. He should have made love to her slowly and tenderly, held her hand and whispered words of love as he did. He should have allowed her time to get used to him, while he eased the pain away. She'd offered him the most precious gift a woman could give a man, and he'd been an animal.

Bailey crawled from his lap and grabbed for her clothes, inching away. He didn't stop her, though he ached to. Clenching his fists at his sides was the only way to keep from pulling her back into his arms. He'd been enough of an animal for one morning.

The look on her face sliced through him, as did the gut-wrenching fact that he'd been the one to put it there. All he knew was that he wanted to gather her into his arms and make her pain go away.

"Bailey, I'm so sorry. I fucked up. This was a mistake. I never should have—"

Her head snapped back and he saw the shocked look in her eyes, actually *heard* her heart breaking. He regretted the words the second they crossed his lips.

"Christ, that's not what I meant!" He ran his hands through his hair, frustrated that he was just making things worse.

* * *

Bailey

Bailey looked away, avoiding his eyes. What was supposed to be one of the best moments of her life had turned into one of the worst. Shame and humiliation enveloped her, made it hard to breathe.

She wanted to crawl under a rock, to disappear from the face of the earth and never be seen again. How could she have been so naïve to think she could handle herself with a man like Michael Connelly? A man who, quite obviously, had believed her to be far more experienced than she was.

She'd wanted it, literally begged him for it, but she hadn't expected it to *hurt* so much.

And it wasn't just the physical pain, it was the way he'd taken her. When they started, she felt like he was right there with her, so skilled, wickedly playing her body and making it sing. But then something happened and he'd changed, taking her with a ferocity she hadn't foreseen, ignoring her cries and pleas to slow down.

In her fantasies, he'd been a gentle, caring lover, with the practical knowledge of sex that she lacked. Taking his time, knowing exactly what she needed, easing her through it. In those dreams, her cries had been those of raging desire, not pain. And they had reached the heights of passion together, then basked in the afterglow, snug in each other's arms.

The reality was so much different than the fantasy. She was blubbering like an idiot schoolgirl, and he looked as if he'd rather be anywhere else. There was nothing romantic about the situation now, just terrible awkwardness. And he was already backtracking, attempting damage control by apologizing and calling it a *mistake*.

The only mistake was her being a naïve fool.

"Come on, I'll take you home."

His deep voice, so filled with regret, was like a blade to the heart. She took a step and felt the uncomfortable burn between her legs, mortified by the smears of red visible in the stark morning light. The thought of straddling the motorcycle seat for a long ride down the mountain was not a pleasant one.

"I – I need a few minutes to, uh, …"

He didn't even look at her as he reached for his clothes, but his profile couldn't hide the hard set to his features "Sure. Take all the time you need."

Grabbing her clothes, she held them up to cover herself as much as possible, then carefully climbed from the ledge and back onto the path, setting a course for the privacy of the trees.

* * *

Michael

"Fucking goddamn it all to hell!"

Michael winced when he saw how gingerly she walked. Christ, he'd brutalized her, and it sickened him.

Damn it, he should be holding her naked in his arms right now as she dozed against his chest, spent and sated from their lovemaking. She should *not* be running away from him in tears, feeling the need to hide herself from him.

Next time, he would be infinitely gentle and tender. He swore to himself that he would never lose control with her like that again. He'd greatly underestimated the power of joining with someone he loved...

The realization hit him like a thunderbolt. He loved her.

Sure, he'd accepted that she was his *croie*, but until that moment, the real truth of it had remained hidden beneath the heavy mantle of desire. Somehow, during those late night visits and topical conversations, she managed to wrap herself around his heart without him knowing.

He heard the sound of splashing beyond the trees, knew that she was trying to wash away the evidence of her shattered innocence, but nothing could erase the truth. Even now the pleasure of that fact roared inside him like some feral beast, and he wondered again what had come over him.

Because with Bailey it was not sex. It was something else entirely; something so powerful it rocked him to his core. From the moment he'd entered her, he had lost control, swept away by the power that came with their joining. He'd given himself up to his baser needs, assuming she was right there with him. There was only the insane, crushing, undeniable need to take her, to make her his own, forever. Bailey was not just another woman, not just a bed partner. She was his mate, the other half of his soul, and the one he would make his wife.

Did she understand this? No, probably not. He didn't quite understand it himself, though somehow, he knew it to be true with every fiber of his being.

He would find a way to explain it to her, because she *had* to know. This was not something either of them could walk away from; that choice had been taken off the table the moment he first saw her. When he had looked into those amazing blue-green eyes and his heart lurched as if it suddenly had been granted a *reason* to beat.

Every time he saw her after that it became increasingly clear that she affected him like no other woman had. He lived to see her face, to hear her voice, even if it was only asking him if he wanted more coffee. He'd discreetly watched her from the corner, increasingly aware of the gentle sway of her hips when she walked and the effect it had on him. Even now, that simple image had him hardening again, especially since he now knew the glory of what lie between those hips.

Christ, he really was a selfish bastard. At that very moment, she was suffering the effects of his savage possession, and all he could think about was how he wanted her again. Now that he'd had her, he knew he would never be satisfied. He would always want her. He would always crave more.

"Fuck!"

Michael rubbed his face with his hands, trying to push back the memory of how it felt to release inside her. To hold back the hungry need to do it again and again. That wasn't what she needed right now, and he had to be what *she* needed, he realized, his very life depended on it.

Another thought flashed through his mind, then, one that had him both elated and terrified at the same time. He *had* released in her. A forceful, substantial release, without a single thought of using protection. It was yet another indication of exactly how far gone he had been.

What if he'd gotten her pregnant? It was a definite possibility. The Connelly men were infamous for being a virile, fertile bunch, which is why he had always taken so many precautions (this morning notwithstanding). He'd been conceived on his parent's wedding night. His mother often joked that Johnny was created with little more than a potent look from his father, and that Celina came along with a suggestive thought. If she hadn't developed complications and had an emergency hysterectomy after Lina was born, he'd probably have a dozen more siblings.

"Son of a fucking bitch!"

Given that Bailey was a virgin, he had to assume that she was not on any kind of birth control. Inexplicably, that pleased him on a basic level. That primitive part of him reared up again at the thought of Bailey carrying his child. If he thought he felt protective before, he was now absolutely obsessed.

He would be asking her to marry him, of course, regardless. That was a certainty. But first, he had to convince her that he was not really the insensitive, lust-driven monster he appeared to be.

That might be tough.

Michael lifted his face to the sky and vowed, to himself and to God, that he would spend the rest of his life making it up to her.

* * *

Bailey

Michael's curses carried on the still morning air. Some words were easily identifiable, others, not as much.

The sex hadn't exactly been what she'd hoped for, but knowing he regretted it so much made her feel even worse.

It had been stupid on her part to romanticize it, no matter how hard she'd fallen for him. She'd been doing such a good job (or so she'd thought) of keeping her feelings hidden, but that was a whole lot easier to do when she was serving him coffee than it was while lying naked beneath him.

She picked her way carefully down the incline, aiming for the shore. The task would have been easier with two free hands and footwear, but she was sufficiently agile enough to make it to the water line without injury.

Another oath rent the silence as she dipped her cami in the cool water and used it to clean the tender area between her legs. She felt a stab of sympathy for him; he probably wasn't used to dealing with situations like this. Given the ferocity of his reaction when he'd realized the truth, most of his hook-ups weren't as inexperienced.

Probably so he could avoid scenes like this one.

Bailey dried herself and carefully slid her damp legs into her jeans. In retrospect, she should have worn something more giving, but it was what it was.

She didn't bother with the soggy cami, opting instead to go with just the button-down. The soft, brushed cotton felt good against her skin, a small comfort at least.

"Bailey!"

Michael's voice called out from somewhere above, probably anxious to be on his way and put this whole morning behind him. That made two of them. The difference was, if she had the chance to set the clock back several hours, she'd probably do the same thing all over again.

Because somewhere along the line, she'd done the unthinkable. She'd fallen in love with him. She should have kept her distance, fantasizing from afar, keeping their relationship to the innocent flirting over coffee and cinnamon rolls. That would have been the smart thing to do.

But no, she'd selfishly allowed it to progress to the next step. In doing so, Michael had transformed from the quiet, unattainable protector to the personification of male sexuality. Everything about him, from his hardened, sculpted body to his sweet, warm breath, promised ecstasy. His skillful touch and masterful kisses had her nearly insane with desire. And the size of him *down there*, well, she didn't have a lot of experience with that sort of thing, but even she knew that wasn't normal. No wonder so many women spoke of him in hushed whispers.

And no doubt every one of them had been a better lover than she had, she thought bitterly.

"Bailey! Where are you? Is everything okay?"

She laughed, a muffled, strangled sound. No, everything *wasn't* okay. But it would be. People couldn't actually die from humiliation, right?

"Give me a minute," she called back. *Or a hundred.* She needed to work up her courage before she faced him again.

Clothed and feeling marginally better, she wrapped her arms around herself and walked farther along the shoreline, breathing in the crisp morning air. The warm rays of the sun felt good, but it wasn't enough to take away the chill that had settled inside her.

The public boat launch was just ahead, a gently sloping expanse of fist-sized white and gray rocks. An older model pick-up truck was backing down, pushing a bass boat and trailer toward the water where an older man waited, guiding the driver with fluid hand signals. His tan fishing hat was studded with feathery lures, just like his vest.

Bailey moved back toward the trees before they

spotted her. Her father used to like early morning fishing, too. When she was little, he'd take her and her siblings on hours-long float trips. Her mother would drop them off, then go wait for them downriver. They spent more time untangling lines than actually fishing, but it had been fun. At the end of their trip, her mom would have a big spread laid out, and they'd eat sandwiches and chips and sip juice on blankets beneath the trees…

She sighed, the familiar sadness settling over her. She missed them so much. They'd been good, loving parents. As kids, they'd never wanted for anything then.

She still had trouble believing how quickly everything had changed. Everything.

The fire that claimed her mother and father had been ruled accidental, but Bailey knew better. She'd seen Simon that night, and knew in her heart that he'd been behind it. Unfortunately, she had no proof, and he had enough officials in his pocket to squash any further investigation. Anyone who tried to prove his involvement in the fire ended up dead.

Or worse. If Simon managed to find her, her fate wouldn't be as kind.

Becoming CEO of her family's multimillion-dollar company wasn't enough. Simon wanted to own it. And for that, he needed *her*.

The dismal thoughts were a grim, though much-needed, reality check. She couldn't afford to wallow in self-pity or lament the impossibility of something more than a quick tumble, not without putting herself and her sisters in danger.

She'd come here with Michael, knowing what would happen, and knowing it was a one-time deal. So what if it hadn't been all fireworks and rose petals? It was what it was. She got what she wanted (more or less), and now it was time to pull up her big girl panties and move on.

She turned to go back up to the ledge, back to Michael, then she hesitated. How was she going to handle this? Did she really want to ride back into town, uncomfortably straddling the back of a motorcycle?

Not really, but it was the quickest and safest way, and the sooner she got back to her place, the sooner she could get out of town.

On the other hand, it would also mean that she'd have to hold on to Michael for the long ride, and that was harder to swallow. Not only would it be awkward, but every time she was around him, her common sense clocked out, and she couldn't afford any more distractions.

Knowing him and his chivalrous tendencies, he probably wouldn't be content to just drop her off and let her go. And then what would she do? Lie and say it was all cool? He'd see through that in a second.

"Bailey!"

Michael's voice called out again, and her heartbeat kicked up a notch. She had to make a decision. Did she go back to Michael and risk another lack of judgment call on her part? Or would it be better to make it a clean break now and run?

chapter eight

Michael

Michael paced back and forth along the small clearing, guilt eating at him like acid. Bailey still hadn't returned. She needed some time, he understood that, but he needed to look into her eyes and see that she was physically unharmed. That she didn't hate the sight of him. To hold her and apologize for losing control until she believed him.

It was too quiet. She'd been out of his sight for too long. He told himself that she was probably just sitting quietly, trying to pull herself together before she faced him again. Despite his rationalizations, worry rode him hard. His gut told him something wasn't right.

"Bailey?" he called. "You okay?" No answer. *Of course she's not okay, you idiot. You made sure of that.*

Concern outweighed the desire to give her some privacy, and he made his way over to where she'd disappeared. Bent branches and flattened scrub revealed the path she had taken down toward the water.

Be calm. She's fine.

The hair prickling on the back of his neck suggested otherwise.

He made it down close to the boat launch, where two older men were just pushing away from shore.

"Excuse me, but have you seen a woman come through here lately?"

The man pushing the boat farther into the water stopped and regarded him for a long minute before he curled his lips, turned his head, and spit tobacco juice into the water. "Barefoot with brown hair?"

"Yeah."

"Yep, we saw her. She asked how far it was to the main road."

Michael's heart froze. "The main road?"

Another look. Another spit. "Said she was camping with her boyfriend and went out for a walk, forgot which way she came, but knew it was close to the road."

What?!

The older man narrowed his eyes. "You the boyfriend?"

Fuck yes, he was. He nodded. "How long?"

"Fifteen minutes, give or take."

Fuck. Fuck. Fuck!

Michael ran across the lot and up the stone-filled access drive to the upper parking lot, then another half a mile or so up to the main road, but there was no sign of Bailey.

She was gone.

By the time he made it back to the boat launch, the two older men were nothing but a speck on the horizon as they motored out across the lake.

What the hell was he going to do now?

He found her footprints in the mud right beyond the trees, saw where she had kneeled to rinse herself off. He found the black silk camisole bunched up into a ball a few feet away, soaking wet and tossed against the base of a tree.

"Bailey," he said into the empty space, "I'm sorry. *Baby, I am so fucking sorry.*"

He fought against the panic threatening to overtake him. There were lots of dangers in these mountains. Copperheads, rattlesnakes, coyotes, bears. Steep, sudden drop-offs and cliffs of shale that could slide out from beneath you without warning. Not to mention the hundreds of footpaths that threaded through the dense forest. Someone unfamiliar with the area could wander around for days and not find their way out. Michael shoved the horrible images out of his head and forced himself to think.

It had to be close to twenty miles to town, down unfamiliar mountainous terrain. She was barefoot and alone. Could she possibly hate him that much to risk it?

After making a thorough search of the area,

Michael didn't like the answer staring him right in the face. He was convinced of two things. One, that she was unhurt (relatively speaking of course, the harm he'd inflicted through his own brutality, notwithstanding), and two, that she had chosen to run away rather than face him. The first conclusion gave him some infinitesimally small measure of comfort and hope. The second left a gaping hole in his heart.

Michael rested his forehead against one of the ancient oaks along the shore. How was he going to fix this? He would never forgive himself if anything happened to her. Fuck his pride, he needed help with this one. Bailey obviously didn't want anything to do with him right now, but it was just too dangerous for her to be wandering these mountains on her own. He slumped down against the trunk and whipped out his mobile, hitting the speed dial.

"Kyle? Yeah, I know what time it is… Yeah, I get it, man… No, I need your help, I really fucked up… Yeah, with Bailey… I'm up here at the lake… No, not the cabin, along the shore… Yeah, that's right… Bailey's run off, she's really pissed and… No, on foot… I don't know, maybe thirty minutes… Yeah, thanks, man."

He disconnected, then hit the speed dial once again. "Stace? Yeah, it's Michael… No, everything is not all right… I need Johnny… yeah, thanks." That conversation went similarly to the previous one, but Johnny was more vocal in his responses than Kyle had been.

Funny, Michael thought, that of the two men he trusted most in this world the first one he called wasn't his brother. Maybe that's because he instinctively knew Kyle would have a better understanding of what he was going through. Kyle had screwed up catastrophically with Lina a year earlier. Back then, Michael could not, for the life of him, understand how Kyle could be so unbelievably clueless when it came to the woman he loved. Now, he understood all too well. And he knew too, that like Kyle, the only way to fix it was to find Bailey and beg her forgiveness.

Fuck. Karma was a bitch.

Michael sighed and slid the phone back into his pocket, then returned to the rock to wait for his brothers. True, Kyle was technically his brother-in-law, but he fit into the family so seamlessly that it was much easier to think of him as a brother.

He folded up the blood-stained blanket, careful that when complete, nothing was visible from the outside. Then he picked up the threaded cup, tossed out the remains of the cold coffee, and screwed it back on top of the steel Thermos. The mindless actions helped him focus, and gave his hands something to do while he waited.

The remains of the cinnamon roll ended up in the trees for some lucky woodland creature to find. With care, he placed it all in Bailey's backpack, including the soft leather boots she'd left behind. He let a string of oaths cross his lips, most of which were in the old Irish tongue of his family. She was wandering around the mountains barefoot, which to his mind, was nothing less than an act of desperation meant to accomplish one thing: to get as far away from him as quickly as possible.

He sighed again and sat down on the rock. It was going to be the longest fucking day of his life.

* * *

Bailey

Bailey sat quietly, safely hidden among the dense foliage of the ancient oak. She'd doubled back for her knapsack, but she'd wasted too much time. Thankfully, she'd heard him before she saw him, and only just managed to get out of sight before he re-entered the clearing. With any luck, he'd just get on his bike and go. Her arms were itching like crazy, making her think she'd hit a patch of poison oak or ivy along the way.

Funny, she thought, how no one ever looked *up.*

What the hell is he waiting for?

Once he was gone, she'd wait a little while longer, then grab her pack and her shoes, slip out the way they came in, and follow the main road toward town. If she was lucky, she'd find a place to catch a few hours of sleep. Then she'd wait until nightfall, sneak into her apartment, and grab the escape kit she kept handy and ready to go at a moment's notice. Thankfully, she hadn't acquired much, so she wouldn't have to leave a lot behind. At least she'd learned that lesson well.

The sound of crunching gravel announced the arrival of someone else. Bailey watched from her perch as a black Land Rover pulled in beside Michael's Harley. Two men exited the vehicle and approached Michael. Bailey recognized them as the same men she'd seen at Tommy's the night before.

She heard the murmur of their voices, but couldn't make out their words.

"How the fuck was I supposed to know?" Michael's raised voice carried up to her. The blonde was poking his finger into Michael's chest and Michael looked as if he was ready to kill him. The blonde guy must have said something else then because Michael lunged for him, and the other dark-haired guy – the one with the mirrored shades – grabbed Michael from behind, pinning his arms and pulling him away from the blonde.

Jeez, he had to be pretty strong to do that, Bailey thought. Michael was no lightweight.

Shades released Michael, and positioned himself between the other two men. He seemed the least hot-headed among them and was trying to get the situation back under control. A few minutes later, Shades patted Michael on the shoulder and said something that had Michael nodding. Goldilocks reached out for Michael's hand and the two of them gave a brotherly chest-bump embrace, leading Bailey to assume that things were cool between them once again. They started walking toward their vehicles when Michael stopped, turned around, and grabbed her backpack.

Damn it!

It wasn't bad enough she had to give up the man she loved, but her favorite backpack, too? And it held her good Thermos. Any thoughts of finishing off the coffee and rolls went right out the window. Her untraceable cell phone, hidden in an inside pocket, was now useless, as was the emergency syringe filled with insulin.

She looked toward the rising sun, trying to gauge the time. She'd be due for another dose in a few hours. Thankfully, she'd remembered to inject herself right before they'd left for the lake.

Michael mounted his cycle, and with one last look around the clearing, kick-started the bike and took off. Shades slid into the black Rover but left the door open. He had a cell phone to his ear for a minute or two before she saw him slide it into his jacket. Goldilocks climbed in the passenger side, then they took off as well.

Bailey sat in the tree for a while longer, just in case any of them happened back. When an hour passed with no returns, she skillfully descended and dropped the last ten feet into a crouch. Then she slowly began making her way out toward the main road and down the mountain, thankful for the density of the forest and the shadows it provided.

chapter nine

Michael

Michael knew that Bailey was running from him, and some logical part of his brain understood that. He needed to find her, beg her forgiveness, and then convince her he wasn't the mindless, rutting beast he'd been on that ridge. Yes, he'd lost control, and no, it wouldn't *ever* happen again.

His Harley was not the quietest machine in the world, and she would no doubt hear him approaching a mile away. It would be easy enough for her to avoid him, but that was okay. At least she would know that he *was* looking for her. He had to get points for trying, right?

He was expecting better results from Kyle and Johnny, however. Bailey wasn't familiar with the Rover. Not that she would flag it down or anything, but at least she'd be less likely to hide from it, and they might have a better chance of spotting her. The Rover also had the added benefits of some excellent off-road capabilities should that become an issue.

The plan was that they would cruise the winding mountain roads until they either found her or until they received word that she made it safely back to town. Lina and Stacey were handling that end of things.

* * *

Bailey

Several hours later, Bailey was seriously questioning the sanity of her plan. She was no stranger to the great outdoors, but hiking down an unfamiliar mountain in bare feet with nothing but the clothes on her back wasn't the brightest idea she'd had. Still, all she had to do was flash a few images through her mind from this morning and she knew she would have made exactly the same decision again.

Yeah, she was running away. But it was what she was best at.

Less than twenty yards away, the Rover cruised by again. That thing had crossed her path at least half a dozen times, and of those, two had been damn close. She must be losing her touch; she was too distracted. She wasn't thinking clearly. Her mind was conspiring against her.

Her heart was in on it, too. Each time she thought about never seeing Michael again, it ached.

Suck it up, cupcake.

Annoyed with herself, she pulled yet more leaves from her hair, a result of the last time she dove behind that huge mass of mountain laurel to avoid being seen. Her skin itched from all the scratches she'd acquired, and the red rash she suspected was poison ivy had now morphed into ugly, fluid-filled bumps. Her feet were cut and bleeding.

To make matters worse, she was tired and hungry and ached all over. She had no food, no water, and nothing in the way of supplies. If she didn't get something in her system soon, she was going to crash and her emergency insulin was in the backpack Michael had taken. Normally she wouldn't need her next dose until nightfall, but that was assuming she'd had enough sleep and a steady supply of food to keep her system stable.

A quick glance skyward revealed the sun directly overhead, streaming in laser-like beams through the foliage. That meant there was about eight hours of daylight remaining, and she was quickly revising her plan to remain in these godforsaken woods until nightfall.

She needed another option.

Her salvation came in the form of a sleek black Jaguar driving fast up the narrow, curvy mountain road. The hard, pounding sounds of rock music blasted through the open windows at full volume, echoing in the stillness and broadcasting its approach well in advance.

Bailey got a quick peek at the driver as the car wove in and out of sight below her current location: Young, female. *Perfect*.

Bailey moved closer to the road. The Rover was out of sight; by her calculations it wouldn't be making another loop around for at least fifteen minutes. As if she had nothing better in the world to do, she strolled along the side of the road, turning when the bass grew louder, and held out her thumb in a classic hitchhiker gesture.

The Jag slowed. Bailey allowed it to pull beside her, though she stayed ready to make a run for it if necessary.

Through the open passenger window, Bailey saw two women. The driver was a woman around her age with golden blonde hair and a pair of dark shades. The woman closest to her was also young, with cherry-brown hair and unusual, silvery gray eyes. Both wore loose-fitting casual clothes and looked like two friends off for a day up at the lake.

The driver turned down the volume and leaned over. "You need a ride, hon?"

Bailey shook her head. The Jag was heading up the mountain toward where she'd come from, not down towards the town. "Do you have a cell phone I could use? "

"I do, but it won't do you any good. Battery's dead. I can never remember to charge the stupid thing."

Bailey nodded, wondering when, and if, she'd

get a break. It was almost as if some unseen force didn't want her to succeed.

The driver tapped a nail against the steering column as if considering something. "My cabin's not too far away. We're headed there now for a little girl time. It's got a landline you could use."

Bailey considered this. A private cabin would afford exactly what she needed, which at this point included a civilized bathroom with toilet paper and a working phone.

"Are you in some kind of trouble or something?" The woman in the passenger seat studied her closely. She looked past Bailey as if she half-expected to see someone running after her with a shotgun. Not seeing anything, she peered down at Bailey's bare feet, one eyebrow cocking in the process.

"Not the kind you're thinking," Bailey said with a look that defied them to think otherwise.

After a couple of awkward moments, the driver's face grinned with a knowing look. "Ah, Stace, I think she's all right. Bet she's got man trouble. Rat bastards, all of 'em. Hop on in, hon, we've got your back."

There was something extremely likable about the driver; Bailey sensed a kindred spirit. The other woman was probably okay, too, just cautious. Bailey certainly couldn't fault her for that. Nor could she reasonably expect a better opportunity to come along anytime soon. Trusting her instincts,

Bailey nodded, and was rewarded with an even bigger grin and the snick of the back door unlocking.

"Hope you like Warrant," the driver said, reaching for the volume control.

"And aren't prone to motion sickness," muttered the passenger with a wry smile.

In another second the volume was turned back up and the Jag shot forward like a rocket.

Oh yeah, Bailey thought with a smile. She liked these two.

Nevertheless, she could not afford to get sloppy. She shrank as far as possible into the back seat and held her breath as the Jag wound its way up the mountain and continued past the turn-off Michael had taken to the lake. Only then did she allow herself to relax slightly. After all, Michael (and anyone else looking for her) would expect her to head toward town, not in the other direction.

The "cabin" turned out to be more like a swanky resort, with beautiful wood, floor-to-ceiling windows, and expensive-looking furnishings. Bailey hesitated at the door, afraid to enter with the state she was in.

"Come on in," the driver said airily. "Believe me, this place has seen a lot worse. You should see what my brothers do up here. By the way, my name's Lina."

"And I'm Stacey," said the one with the cherry-brown hair. She walked with the aid of two canes strapped to her forearms. Bailey flushed when Stacey caught her eyeing them.

"Learning to walk again," Stacey explained matter-of-factly. "A bad accident had me in a wheelchair for a long time, so this is like a tiptoe through the tulips to me."

"I'm sorry, I didn't mean to stare." Bailey said, embarrassed.

"Don't sweat it, sweetie," Stacey told her with a smile.

It was too bad Bailey hadn't met these two earlier. She had a feeling they might have been friends, and she definitely could have used some of those over the past few months. Unfortunately, Bailey's nomadic lifestyle didn't afford much opportunity for things like BFFs.

Or boyfriends.

Lina set her bag down in the living room and tossed her keys on the counter. "Phone's in there," she said, pointing toward a small alcove next to the kitchen area. "You're welcome to hang out here a bit if you'd like. You look like you could use a shower and a change of clothes." Lina looked her up and down appraisingly. "I'm sure we can find something that'll work for you, plus we've got some awesome stuff that'll help with that poison."

"I don't think—" Bailey started to protest, but Lina cut her off with a wave of her hand.

"Whatever. Offer stands. Did I mention there's a hot tub?"

Oh, now *that* sounded nice. Easing her aching body into hot, bubbling water and spending the rest of the day there. But like so many things, it was a luxury in which she would not indulge. Now a shower – preferably with some grease-cutting dishwashing liquid to dissolve the poisonous oils on her skin – that was doable.

"Do you mind if I grab one of those?" Bailey asked, indicating the bag of Clementines Lina had just dropped on the counter. The fruit would help regulate her sugar levels, which were becoming increasingly out of whack.

"Sure thing. Help yourself." Bailey caught the orange Stacey lobbed at her with a deft one-handed grab. Without bothering to peel it, Bailey bit into it like an apple, leaning against the counter for support. It did not go unnoticed by either woman.

"Stace, see what we've got in the fridge, will you? I'm starving."

Stacey dutifully peered into the stainless steel side-by-side. "Hmmm. Bacon, eggs, looks like some of those biscuits you pop in the oven…"

"Mmmmm. Yes, yes, and yes." Lina laughed.

"Want to join us for brunch?" Stacey asked Bailey, lining things up on the counter. "There's enough here to feed a small army."

Bailey was just about to decline when her stomach growled loudly, yet another organ betraying her.

Lina laughed. "We'll take that as a yes. Come

on, I'll show you where the bathroom is while Stace starts breakfast."

Lina walked across the kitchen, beckoning Bailey to follow. When she didn't, Lina turned around.

"Maybe it's none of my business, but you look like you could use a little help right now. We're offering you a hot shower, a change of clothes, a kick-ass breakfast – Stace is a phenomenal cook, by the way - and a place to chill for a while, no questions asked. You can take us up on it, or you can make your phone call and be on your way. Your choice."

Bailey was shocked at Lina's openness. Noticing her expression, Stacey chuckled. "Yeah, she's like that. Subtle as a Mack truck. You get used to it after a while."

"Why would you do all that for me?" Bailey asked with genuine curiosity. "You don't even know me."

"So tell me your name."

Bailey bit her lip. "Bailey."

"Nice to meet you, Bailey. You already know our names, so that takes care of that. And as to the 'why' of it, well, does it really matter?"

Bailey considered this for a moment, then a slow grin spread across her face. Why look a gift horse in the mouth? Usually, people were overly curious; digging places they had no business digging. These women were offering what amounted to sanctuary, no questions asked. Too good to be true, perhaps, but it wasn't like beggars could be choosers. Besides, by the looks of them, they were no threat to her.

"No," Bailey said finally. "I guess it doesn't."

"Great! Glad we got that out of the way. Now come on, you're going to love the double shower heads."

* * *

Lina

Lina eyed Bailey again, nodding her head when she confirmed she and Bailey were about the same size. She picked out a pair of comfortable shorts and a soft tank and left Bailey in the bathroom with everything she needed. Scooping up Bailey's clothes with the intent of throwing them in the washer, she headed back out to the kitchen.

Stacey held her cell phone out to her and mouthed, "It's Michael."

Lina shifted the bundle and took the phone, keeping her voice low. She didn't want to chance Bailey overhearing.

"Yeah, we got her... She's in the shower now... A couple of scratches and scrapes, and a nice case of poison oak, but otherwise she looks okay... No, I don't think that's a good idea. Give us a few hours, okay?... Yeah, go home and get some sleep. Tell

Kyle and Johnny to stay away too. We've got things covered… You're welcome, Michael… Love you, too. Don't worry."

Stacey put a tray of rolls into the oven and closed the door. "Is she going to be okay?"

"I don't know. She's like a scared rabbit or something. One slip and she's going to bolt, I know it. I wish I knew more about what happened. I feel like I'm driving blind here."

"Michael didn't tell you anything?" Stacey's voice was unusually quiet and serious, and her eyes were locked on the bundle of clothes in Lina's hands.

"Just that he screwed up somehow and Bailey took off. Why?"

Stacey's eyes met Lina's. "Because Bailey's clothes have blood stains on them, Lina."

Lina looked down and gasped. "Oh, Stace. This is so not good."

"Quick, put them back before she knows we saw them."

"Right." Lina disappeared and returned empty handed a minute later. She saw the expression on Stacey's face and shook her head. "No, Stace, don't even think that. Michael would never hurt a woman intentionally. He would die first."

"I'm sorry, Lina, I know that. But I have to admit, hearing you say it makes me feel better. What are we going to do?"

Lina bit her lip. "I don't know. I do know that

I've never seen Michael like this, which means we have to help them work this out. I guess we'll play it by ear and see what happens."

* * *

Michael

Michael sagged in relief once he hung up with Lina. Bailey was safe at the cabin and they would watch over her. As much as his gut was urging him to head up there at that moment, he knew Lina was right. He should keep his distance until Lina and Stacey worked their feminine magic and got a proper read on the situation.

He called Kyle and Johnny to give them the update then headed back into town.

A couple of hours, Lina had said. Hopefully enough time for him to figure out a way to fix this mess. To find some way to explain the inexcusable. "I'm sorry, I got carried away" wasn't going to cut it, no matter how true that was. From the moment he'd entered her, he'd been lost. The sheer intensity that came from joining with his *croie* had been unexpected, launching a full and brutal assault on the last threads of his already-thin control.

Now that he knew what to expect, he would make damn sure it never happened again.

Michael sighed. Maybe he should just be honest with Bailey. Lay bare his soul and pray she was willing to listen. It had worked for Kyle, after all.

The only thing he knew for sure was that he *would* fix this, because being without her was not an option.

chapter ten

Bailey

"Feeling better?" Lina asked brightly when Bailey emerged from the shower a little later, wearing the clothes that had been laid out for her.

"Yes, thanks. Um, did I hear you mention you've got a washer and dryer here?" Bailey held the clothes she'd been wearing earlier protectively in a tight bundle against her chest.

"Yep. Through that pantry door, on the left. Help yourself."

When Bailey returned a few minutes later, she sniffed appreciatively. "That smells wonderful! Can I help?"

"Sure," Stacey said. "Grab those rolls out of the oven. The mitt's on the counter there."

They ate in relative silence, until Lina sat back and patted her belly in satisfaction. "You're too good a cook, Stace. I feel like a total pig."

Stacey beamed, obviously pleased. "Glad you

liked it. At least we got something in you today."

No sooner were the words out of her mouth than Lina pushed herself away from the table and sprinted for the bathroom.

"Or not..." Stacey said, reaching for her arm canes. Bailey beat her there, and was attempting to hold Lina's hair behind her while she vomited violently into the toilet. When it looked like she was done, Bailey wet a washcloth and held it to Lina's face.

"All day morning sickness, huh?"

"Yeah, how'd you guess?" Lina offered a weak smile. "Thanks, by the way. You saved me from having to wash my hair again today."

"I swear, Lina, we're going to have to hook you up to an I.V. soon if you don't start keeping some food down." Stacey leaned against the doorway, concern etching her features.

Lina reached up for the bottle of mouthwash on the sink, poured some into her hand, then swished it around in her mouth and spit into the toilet. "Lots of women have morning sickness, Stace. I refuse to be a whiner about it."

"Not like this, Lina. You're supposed to be putting on weight, not losing it. How much have you lost already?"

When Lina didn't answer, Stacey said quietly, "What does your husband say?"

Lina shot her a warning glance. "He's ready to call 911 when I get a hangnail, Stacey. And compared to what you've gone through, this is a walk in the park. *Let it go.*"

Stacey drew her lips together in a tight line but said nothing. Bailey had the impression a lot more would have been said on the subject if she hadn't been around.

"I'm going to see if the washer's done yet," she said, backing out of the room.

* * *

Stacey

"Let me call Kyle to come and get you," Stacey said quietly once Bailey had gone. "You should be at home, in bed, where he can take care of you and wait on you like the little princess you are."

Lina cracked a weary smile. "I'm fine. *Really*. Besides, we've got a bigger problem to deal with right now. I've never seen Michael like this over a woman, which means she's probably going to become our sister-in-law – but only if we fix this. Come on. You can make me some tea and we'll see if I can hold down a few saltines, okay?"

* * *

Bailey

The atmosphere was more subdued than it had

been. Lina sat quietly on the sofa with her feet up, sipping tea and nibbling on saltines, while Stacey watched over her with the sharp eyes of a mother hen. Bailey curled up in the oversized armchair, tucking her legs beneath her. Now that she had showered, eaten, and slathered her arms with lotion, she felt much better.

Lina and Stacey said they'd be heading back to town later, and offered to give her a ride. After much thought, Bailey agreed to hang out until then. She felt safe here, and without cash, her only other option was hoofing it wilderness-style. Besides, it was better to conserve her energy until she could get back to her place.

She almost squealed in delight when she saw the latest Salienne Dulcette novel on the table beside her.

"I can't believe it! This isn't even in stores yet! How did you get it? It's supposed to be her hottest one yet!"

Lina flashed a knowing smile at Stacey. "Are you a fan?"

"Oh, yeah, I love her books." Then her face clouded over. "Too bad it's all fantasy."

"You don't believe in soul mates?" Stacey leaned forward in interest.

Bailey sighed. "I used to. But I'm getting too old to believe in fairy tales."

"Like what?" Stacey was really interested now.

"Well, take all that stuff about how magical

your first time is supposed to be, for example. Lies. All of it. It hurts like hell." She bit her lip, suddenly afraid she'd said too much, but Stacey didn't seem to think so.

"Yes," Stacey said slowly, drawing out the word. "It can hurt a lot. But a good man stays with you through the pain, helps you past it. But, to be fair, he can't do that if he's not *aware* of it."

Bailey's eyes were intense. "But he would have to know, wouldn't he? I mean, experienced men, like the ones in those books, always know, don't they?"

"Not necessarily," Stacey said. "Especially if they let themselves get carried away."

"That's true," Lina piped in. "And some men don't believe virgins exist past the age of twenty-one anymore. My husband didn't, until I proved him wrong."

Bailey's eyes widened. "And did it, you know, hurt a lot when you finally did?"

Lina smiled. "Oh yeah. Of course, I don't think it helped that my husband is… well, there's no delicate way to put this… um, shall we say… hung like a horse?"

Stacey snorted and Bailey nearly choked on her tea.

"But he knew that I was, so he took a lot of extra care to make it easier for me. And that made all the difference in the world."

Stacey was nodding her head emphatically.

"Yes! That's it exactly! You see, it's not the great sex that makes Salienne Dulcette's books so well-liked. It's the love stories behind the sex that really appeal to people."

"And you really believe that this stuff actually happens in real life?" Bailey waved the book in the air.

"Yes, I do," Stacey told her, with a twinkle in her eye.

Lina was smiling as well. "That book you are holding right now, in fact, is based on Salienne's own personal love affair with her husband. It's a great read. Why don't you keep it?"

Bailey's mouth dropped open when she lifted the front cover and saw the inscription written there. *To Lina, who never gave up on me, I love you, Salienne.*

"This is a signed first-edition dedicated to … you?" Lina nodded. "Oh. My. God. You actually *know* Salienne Dulcette?"

"Yep. We were roommates in college."

"Then I *definitely* can't accept this. It's made out to you."

"I think if I explain the situation, she'd be willing to send me another. We're quite close."

"I don't know what to say."

"Say you won't give up on true love just yet."

* * *

Michael

Michael was so wound up, he didn't think he'd be able to fall asleep, but the past two days had taken their toll. After grabbing something to eat and taking a long, hot shower, he stretched out on the bed. He was out shortly after his head hit the pillow. Images of Bailey filled his dreams.

He only slept a few hours, but it was all he needed. He spotted Bailey's backpack and thought he should at least toss the blanket in the washing machine. The camisole too. It briefly occurred to him that women's delicates should probably be washed differently than a blanket, but what the hell did he know? He'd buy her a new one if he ruined it. Probably several, in fact, because she looked so damn sexy in them.

He pulled out the blanket and threw it in the washer along with some detergent and hit the button. Then he removed the Thermos, took it over to the sink, and rinsed it out. The edge of the bag caught and it tumbled off the table, spreading the rest of its contents across the floor.

Michael cursed softly. The last thing he needed was to break any of her stuff. He picked up a tiny bottle of saline and a contact lens case. *She wore contact lenses?* A brush. A kerchief. He found the cell phone where it slid under the chair and set it carefully on the table. His eyebrows raised at the sheathed blade he picked up. Removing it from its scabbard he saw that it was exquisitely carved with Celtic and Gaelic symbols. He let out a soft whistle. *Serious stuff.*

A small rectangular pack caught his eye. It turned out to be a disposable syringe pre-filled with insulin. *Oh, hell. She was diabetic?* A quick glance at the dosage and he could see she wasn't a severe diabetic, but also understood that she probably had to watch her diet carefully and maintain a steady schedule of injections.

He grabbed his cell and called Lina at the cabin. Dusk was settling, and he was going up for her. He held the phone to his ear as he put the insulin carefully into his jacket pocket. She must be due for another dose by now.

He cursed again when Lina's cell went right to voicemail. Before he got the phone back into his pocket it rang. He snatched it up, thinking it was Lina, but heard Johnny's voice instead.

* * *

Bailey

Bailey must have dozed off, because the next thing she knew, the room was dim and Stacey was shaking her awake. The contact lenses stuck to her eyes, and she blinked furiously to get them hydrated again.

"Bailey, wake up." It took her a few moments

to remember where she was.

"Do you know how to drive a stick?"

"What?" Bailey tried to brush away the mental cobwebs from her deep sleep.

"Can you drive a stick shift?" Stacey repeated.

"Yes."

"Good. Now listen to me carefully, because we don't have a lot of time. Lina is sick, and I've got to get her to the ER. I can't drive quite yet. I can call her husband to come get her, but we'll save a lot of time if you can drive us to the hospital and he meets us there. Will you help us?"

Bailey answered without hesitation. "Of course. Where is she?"

Lina was sitting by the door, looking very pale. She held a towel by her mouth, and Bailey saw that it was spotted with blood.

Lina gave her a weak smile. "I'm sorry, hon."

"Don't be silly," Bailey said, placing Lina's arm around her shoulder and lifting her up. By the time Stacey made it out to the Jag, Lina was curled up in the back seat and Bailey was behind the wheel, ready to go.

Stacey whipped out a cell phone and spoke into it as they pulled out onto the road. "Lina's sick… We're on our way to the ER now… No, Bailey's driving… Get Kyle and just meet us there, okay? Right. Bye." Stacey held the phone tightly in her hand. Her expression was strained when she turned to Bailey.

"Her husband is going to meet us there. Kyle's going to flip out. Lina wasn't exaggerating when she said he worries about her. "

Bailey didn't know what to say to that, so she remained silent and concentrated on the task at hand. The Jag handled like a dream under her control. As she took yet another turn expertly, she felt Stacey staring at her.

"What?" Bailey cast Stacey a quick sideways glance.

"Thanks."

Bailey gave her a little smile. "Thank me when we get there."

Lina's husband was waiting at the Emergency Room entrance when Bailey pulled the Jag into the lot. His hand was on the door before she even killed the engine. Bailey sucked in a breath, recognizing him as the large, dark-haired man with mirrored shades she'd seen with Michael.

"It's okay," Stacey assured her. "That's Kyle."

Kyle didn't even spare her a glance. His full attention was on Lina.

"What happened, Stacey?" Lina was in his arms and he was moving into the emergency entrance. Stacey was right behind him, struggling to keep up as she explained the situation.

Bailey didn't follow. Things had taken a bizarre turn, and now that she'd done what she could to help, it was time to skedaddle before things got even weirder.

Bailey bent down to put the keys under the floor mat when her door suddenly opened. "I'll take those." Bailey looked up... and up... past the massive chest and into the face of the golden-haired man she'd also seen that morning. Bailey got out of the car slowly and put the keys in his hand.

She heard the rumble of the Harley approaching. Goldilocks looked at her with familiar, luminous green eyes. Bailey stepped backward along the car; he made no move to stop her.

"He's in love with you, you know." He said it so quietly she wasn't sure she'd heard him right. Bailey blinked once before taking off in a full sprint into the shadows just as the Harley came around the corner.

He pocketed the keys and closed the driver side door.

"Lina's already inside?" Michael asked. Goldilocks nodded.

"Bailey drove her in, didn't she?"

"Yeah."

"She's gone?"

"Yeah."

"Fuck."

"Yeah."

Goldilocks threw an arm around Michael's shoulders and they walked together into the building.

Bailey watched from the shadows as the two men disappeared into the bright lights of the ER entrance, shaking her head as realization dawned. *So Lina and Stacey were part of it, too.*

She couldn't really be too angry with them, though. She liked both women, and whatever the reason, they *had* helped her.

As she turned and took off, she genuinely hoped Lina would be okay.

chapter eleven

Bailey

The first thing Bailey did was head back to her apartment. She changed into black jeans and a black shirt, laced up her black Doc Martens, grabbed her leather jacket and her emergency bag and was out the door in less than five minutes. She'd kept her rent paid three months in advance so she didn't feel too bad about skipping out. She taped a prepared envelope with a pre-written apology just inside the door and slipped quietly down the stairs.

The next thing she did was stop by the diner to offer a personal apology to Mr. O'Leary for having to leave him short-handed without notice, but Alyssa informed her that he'd just left for the hospital, having received a call that his pregnant granddaughter had just been rushed to the ER.

"Well, I'll be damned," Bailey murmured. *Conlan O'Leary was Lina's grandfather.* Which meant that he was probably Michael's as well. She couldn't help but smile just a little. She'd been surrounded by their family the whole time and she'd never even known it.

She handed the sealed envelope to Alyssa, gave her an impulsive and totally unexpected hug, and was off again before Alyssa could process what had just happened.

With a deep breath and an ache in her heart, Bailey said goodbye to Birch Falls and melted into the shadows, blending in with the skill developed over too many years of practice, and disappeared.

* * *

Michael

The waiting room seemed unusually small with Michael, Johnny, and Kyle pacing around. Stacey sat quietly in the corner, folding and refolding a flyer she'd found on top of the magazines. Conlan alternated between sitting next to her, holding her hand and pacing the floor with the others.

Michael was torn between going after Bailey and being there for his baby sister. It was a hell of a thing, but he wasn't leaving until he knew Lina and his little niece or nephew were going to be okay.

After what seemed like an eternity, a doctor came out to speak with them. Everyone stood, anxious for news.

"Mr. McCullough?"

Kyle stepped forward, rigid with tension.

"I'm Dr. Samuelson. Your wife is resting comfortably. We'll be moving her upstairs to a semi-private room shortly."

"Is she okay? What about the baby? Can I see her?"

"Relax, Mr. McCullough," the doctor said with a calming smile. "Both are doing fine. Your wife is suffering from severe dehydration and a rupture of the esophagus, most likely a result of chronic vomiting. We've got I.V. fluids and anti-nausea meds going into her now. She says she's been having severe bouts of morning sickness?"

Kyle nodded. "Yes, except it's not just in the morning. She hasn't been able to keep anything down. Her doctor told her it was normal and it would pass."

A dark look crossed over Dr. Samuelson's face, as if he didn't agree. Michael was right there with him on that. "With a special diet and some anti-nausea medication, the rest of the pregnancy should progress without incident."

"Can I see her now?"

"Please. She's been asking for you." Dr. Samuelson smiled wryly. "I believe she offered to show me a new place to put my stethoscope if I didn't let you in soon."

Kyle smiled and everyone in the waiting room laughed, releasing some of the tension that had been riding them hard. "Then I suggest you point me in the right direction, Doc, because my wife is not one to issue idle threats."

Assured that Lina was in good hands, the others filed out into the cool night air a short time later. Conlan insisted they all head down to the diner. Michael promised to catch up with them there and made a quick trip to Bailey's apartment first, on the off chance she was hiding out there.

She wasn't.

Eleven o'clock came and went, and Bailey didn't show for her shift. Michael knew in his heart she'd already gone. Conlan seemed to know it, too.

"I'm going to miss that lass," Conlan said. "Assuming, of course, that someone doesn't get off his sorry arse and bring her back where she belongs, that is." He looked pointedly at Michael.

"*Daideo*," Michael said heavily, "it's more complicated than that."

"Bah!" the old man snorted. "Do you love her?"

"*Daideo*—"

"Do. You. Love. Her? It's a simple question. It deserves a simple answer."

Michael clenched his jaw. "Yes, but—"

The old man's fist pounded hard into the table, startling them all. "Damn it, lad! You said it yourself, you were going to make her your bride! I can't for the life of me fathom how any man would be willing to throw away a chance at that kind of happiness, much less a Connelly man."

Michael was stunned at the vehemence with which his grandfather spoke. He looked to Johnny for support, surprised to see him nodding his head in agreement.

"He's right, Mike. You saw Kyle tonight, man. He would die if anything ever happened to Lina or the baby. And nothing in this world could keep me from Stacey. When there was a chance I could lose her…"

Johnny broke off, unable to voice the rest, even now. Michael knew he was referring to the experimental surgery she'd had and the complications that resulted from it. His brother had been a basket case for weeks, refusing to leave her side.

"But you didn't," Stacey reminded Johnny. "And now you are stuck with me forever."

Johnny kissed her passionately, and for several moments they were lost in a world of their own. When Johnny finally released her, Stacey's eyes were dazed.

"*That*'s what I'm talking about," Conlan said approvingly, pinning his eyes on Michael once more. "Did Bailey look like that after you kissed her?"

Yeah, she had, Michael thought, remembering how she, too, had hesitated, mouth slightly parted, eyes unfocused, as if she'd temporarily forgotten where she was.

"That's what I thought. Now, how are we going

to get her back where she belongs?"

"It might be harder than you think, *Daideo*," Stacey said slowly. "I don't think Bailey's like other women."

"Well of course she's not, lass," the older man scoffed. "What would a Connelly man want with some ordinary woman?"

"What do you mean, love?" Johnny asked.

"I think there's more to Bailey than any of us realized. I get the impression that she's, well, running from something."

Conlan and Michael shared a knowing look. Stacey was too shrewd to miss it. "You already knew that, though, didn't you?" She didn't wait for an answer before continuing. "You should have seen her tonight. She was a completely different person – confident and in charge. She practically carried Lina to the car with one arm. She drove that Jag like she'd been born in the seat, and we were hauling *ass* down that mountain."

She gave them a minute to digest that. "And don't you think it's strange that three men who grew up in these mountains, one of them an Army Ranger, were unable to track her, or find the slightest clue as to her whereabouts? I'm telling you, Bailey knows how *not* to be found, and that's not normal."

Just then Alyssa came bustling over to them, holding something in her hand. "I forgot to give this to you when you came in, Mr. O'Leary. Bailey was in earlier and left this for you."

Conlan wasted no time in tearing off the end. A small index card fell out, along with a handwritten note. He scanned it quickly, then read it out loud.

> *Dear Mr. O'Leary,*
>
> *Thank you so much for all of your kindness. You opened your doors and your heart to me, and I will never forget that. You are a very special man, and I will miss you.*
>
> *I wish I could explain why I have to leave so suddenly, but you are a nice man and I don't want to lie to you. Of all the places I've been, I think I will miss Birch Falls the most - for its beauty and charm to be sure, but mostly because of people like you.*
>
> *Try not to worry about me, sir. Despite appearances to the contrary, I do know what I'm doing.*
>
> Go raibh míle maith agat,
> B

"What did that phrase at the end mean? Was that Irish?" Stacey asked.

"Aye. It is an old way of saying thank you. Loosely translated, it means something like 'may you have a thousand good things'. I haven't heard it in years."

"She speaks the Irish then? No wonder you like her so much, *Daideo*," Johnny observed with the hint of a smirk.

"What's on the card?" Stacey asked, pointing to the rectangle that had fallen out of the envelope.

Conlan picked it up and smiled. "It's the recipe for her cinnamon rolls."

"Better hold on to that, *Daideo*," Johnny teased. "Wouldn't want that getting into the wrong hands."

Conlan grinned even wider and handed him the card. Johnny's mouth dropped. It was written in Gaelic.

"Michael Seamus Connelly," Conlan O'Leary said with a twinkle in his eye, "if you don't find that woman and marry her, *I* will."

His grandfather was right. What the hell was he doing sitting here? Bailey was his *croie*, goddamn it, and he *was* going to find her and straighten this shit out once and for all.

"Let's go, *Daideo*, and grab your rental keys."

"Why?"

"Because we're going to find out what the hell's going on, and this way, you won't have to replace the locks afterward."

* * *

Michael

Michael was silent as he worked his way through Bailey's apartment. The place was immaculate. Not a speck of dust or dirt anywhere. A few bottles of water were in the fridge, along with some vanilla soy milk and some vegetarian entrees in the freezer. Michael smiled at the single box of Count Chocula in the cupboard. One dish, one mug, and one fork sat in the draining tray beside the sink. It was all very lonely.

Michael started walking toward the bedroom as Conlan O'Leary moved toward the desk in the living room.

Clearly, this was where Bailey had spent most of her time. A beautifully crafted quilt in various shades of green covered the bed. Stacks upon stacks of books were piled all over the room. Most were romance novels, Michael noted with some amusement, including a huge collection of Salienne Dulcette. He wondered if Bailey knew she'd spent the day with the author, not realizing that Salienne Dulcette was the pen name of Stacey Connelly.

The closet was half-full, mostly with conservative, practical clothes, but it didn't matter what she wore. Bailey could make a brown paper bag look sexy. His eyebrows did raise at the slinky emerald green mini-dress he found in the back. He held it up, picturing how the hem would barely cover her ass and how the deep V-cut would flirt with her navel. He decided that no matter what, he *would* see Bailey in that dress.

Michael sat down on the bed and looked around. Her presence was strong in here. He held her pillow to his face and inhaled. Her sweet, warm scent filled his nostrils and he closed his eyes. His grandfather had been right. He would do anything to have Bailey in his arms again. And once he did, he would never let go.

Michael replaced the pillow and stood up. He walked casually to the window and looked out. A small shadow behind the curtains drew his attention. Upon closer inspection, he found a rope attached to a folding grappling hook and a pair of gloves. Seeing it for what it was – an emergency escape – only heightened his sense of urgency. Bailey wasn't just running from him, she was running from whatever had brought her to Birch Falls in the first place.

She was still in danger. That shit was going to stop, sooner rather than later. Once he found her – and he *would* find her – he was going to eliminate that threat once and for all and make sure she never felt unsafe again.

In the interest of thoroughness, he checked out the bathroom next, but found nothing to help him find her. Body wash, shampoo. Toothbrush, toothpaste (cinnamon flavor). A fluffy white microfiber robe, hanging from the hook.

The place was clean. And he was no closer to

finding her than he'd been an hour ago.

"I think it's time to give Ian a call," Conlan suggested quietly, as he stood in the doorway.

***

Michael

Ian Callaghan was one of Michael's cousins. He lived above the family-owned pub across the river in Pine Ridge, and was known for his knack for unearthing any kind of information, no matter how deeply it was buried, or by whom.

That was how Michael found himself walking into Jake's Irish Pub the next morning.

"Hey, Mikey, good to see you," Jake greeted with a grin. Jake was the second born of his seven cousins and had taken over ownership of the pub from his father, Jack. "Long time no see."

"Yeah," Michael grinned back. It had only been a couple of months since Johnny's wedding. "The place is looking good."

"Thanks. You probably haven't seen it since the latest reno. But that's not why you're here, is it?" Jake asked, giving him a knowing look.

"Is Ian around?"

Jake nodded, thumbing toward the private kitchen. "He's in there, grabbing some coffee."

"Rough night?"

"Worse," Jake grinned. "Woman troubles."

Michael laughed, feeling the truth of his cousin's words. His gut hadn't been this twisted in, well, ever. "That makes two of us."

He walked into the kitchen to find Ian brooding at the table. At Michael's entrance, Ian lifted his gaze and smoothed his features into a mask Michael knew all too well.

"Mike! What's up, man?"

"Ian. I was hoping you could help me out. I need some intel."

Ian sat up in interest. His gaze sharpened. "Anything for you, cuz, you know that. What do you need?"

"Anything you can find on a woman that worked for *Daideo*. She goes by the name of Bailey Keehan, but I'm pretty sure that's not her real name."

A dark eyebrow lifted. "Purely business?"

"No, man. As personal as it gets."

Ian nodded then stood. "Right then. Come on up, and grab that pot of coffee. Oh, and be quiet," he grinned mischievously. "If you wake up Jake's wife Taryn, she'll kick your ass."

Michael followed him up to the third floor, taking in the dizzying display of digital equipment that took up more than half the room. Ian pointed to a rolling chair beside the desk and flexed his fingers. He typed in a series of passwords, then said, "Okay, tell me what you have."

Michael told him what he knew. When she

started working at the diner, the cash-based rental agreement. To his credit, Ian didn't bat an eye; he just kept tapping the keys at a blurring speed. Michael went on to mention "Robert White" and the incident at Tommy's, which did elicit a slight frown.

"That's fucked up. Got a picture?"

Michael nodded and pulled out his phone, bringing up a few shots he'd captured of Bailey at the diner shortly after *Daideo* had called him in.

"Awesome." Ian touched the phone to some kind of scanner, and within seconds, Bailey's images filled the screen.

"I've got some new facial recognition software I've been playing with. If she's ever had her picture taken – like a driver's license or a school yearbook or something – we should get a hit. I'm going to start with the east coast, but if that doesn't turn up anything, I'll expand the search. Could take a day, maybe several, depending on how far out we have to go."

Ian tapped a few keys and sat back. "Any distinguishing features? And I don't mean hair or eye color – those things are easily changeable."

"She's got a couple of tatts."

"Perfect. Tatts are like signatures. Fingerprints, if they're unique enough. Tell me about them."

Michael did him one better. He sketched out a rough picture. An artist, he wasn't, but he was good enough to create a reasonable facsimile.

"A *luckenbooth*, huh?" Ian mused, feeding the paper into yet another machine. "Never seen one before, which is a good thing, because that will narrow down the playing field. Anything else?"

"She's diabetic. Enough that she kept insulin syringes in her backpack."

"Excellent. Anything medical means records. What about family? Did she ever mention a name in passing? If she had any siblings? Whether or not her parents are still living?"

"No," Michael shook his head, thinking back over the last two months. For as many times as they'd spoken, she was careful never to reveal anything personal. Except once, when her guard was way, way down.

"She said her dad was Scottish and her mom was Irish," Michael said. "It's not much, I know."

Ian grinned. "More than I usually have to start with. I'll call you when I have something, yeah?"

"Yeah. Thanks, man."

"Anytime." His eyes twinkled with mischief. "Now... let's go pound on Taryn's door. I'm getting hungry, and the woman makes some damn fine pancakes. But be prepared to run like hell…"

* * *

Bailey

Bailey blended in with the small throng of

people climbing aboard the Greyhound bus. Her hair was a good deal shorter than it had been a few hours ago, coming down only to a few inches below her shoulders – and poker straight, thanks to the flat iron she'd purchased in the Walmart a few miles away. No doubt the humidity would have her hair curling again, but she'd be okay for the next few hours.

An older woman sat next to her. Thankfully, after showing Bailey pictures of her grandchildren, the woman spent the rest of the ride napping, leaving Bailey to her thoughts.

She never thought it would be so hard to leave, but it was. From the moment she'd stepped off the bus in Birch Falls, it had felt like the kind of place she could be happy. Walking away from Michael was even harder. Yeah, it probably wouldn't have lasted long anyway, but it would have been nice to try. He was the only man who had made her seriously question her life choices, and that was saying something.

While Michael was the biggest part of it, he wasn't the only one who made leaving Birch Falls difficult. Conlan O'Leary had treated her like one of his own. Lina and Stacey had, too. Oh, Bailey knew now they'd done what they had more for Michael than her, but the kindness they'd extended felt genuine. They were clearly a close-knit family, one that cared for each other deeply.

Her family had been like that once, too.

By the time they pulled into the bus station in Endicott, NY, she couldn't stand it any longer. She picked up the non-traceable phone she'd purchased the same time she'd gotten the straightener, and dialed the number of the Birch Falls hospital to inquire about Lina. It was a sign of how small the community was when the hospital operator patched her right through to Lina's room. A low, male voice responded on the other end.

"Hello?"

It caught Bailey off guard.

"Hello?" the voice said again. An image of the dark-haired man in shades came into her mind.

"Kyle?"

"Yeah. Who's this?"

"Is Lina okay?"

Kyle paused. "She's okay, Bailey. She's sleeping."

"And the baby?"

"Fine. They're both fine." Bailey released the breath she'd been holding.

"Good. That's good."

"She was asking about you, Bailey. She's worried about you."

Bailey smiled into the phone, once again thinking how, if things had been different, she and Lina and Stacey might have been friends. "You tell her to take care of herself and that baby. And that I said thanks for helping me out. Okay?"

"No."

"Excuse me?"

"I said, no. You can come here and tell her yourself. And while you're at it maybe you can tell that sorry son-of-a-bitch brother of hers that you forgive him so his heart can start beating again."

The silence stretched between them. "What did you say?"

"You heard me."

She'd heard him, but the words didn't make sense.

"Michael thinks I'm angry with him?"

"Aren't you?"

An announcement came over the speakers mounted around the station, loud enough to be heard over the din: *Attention travelers. Greyhound #534 to Watkins Glen is now leaving. All passengers to Watkins Glen, please have your tickets ready and prepare to board.*

"I have to go now, Kyle. Tell Lina I'll be thinking about her."

"Think about what I said. And Bailey?"

"Yeah?"

"Thanks."

"For what?"

"For getting Lina to the hospital so quickly."

"Glad I could help."

* * *

Kyle sighed as she ended the connection. Then

he dialed Michael's number.

After thanking Kyle, Michael called Ian, relaying the new information. Then he packed his duffel, tossed it into his truck, and hit the road. Destination: Watkins Glen, New York.

chapter twelve

Bailey

Bailey sighed, boarding yet another bus. She was really beginning to hate busses. But planes and trains were such a hassle these days. Too many security checks, too many cameras. Nobody gave you a second glance if you took a bus.

She pulled her hair tightly against her head and tucked it up so that it was nearly invisible under the dark hoodie. Her eyes were a burnished gold today, rimmed in dark brown liner. She kept her face buried in a book while surreptitiously remaining aware of everyone and everything around her. She couldn't wait until she could take a deep breath without the stench of diesel fumes and stale body odor.

Several weeks of circuitous routes and multiple coach changes later, she emerged looking somewhat worse for wear in a small town in eastern Kentucky. The first thing she did was hit the local drugstore, pick up some fragrant body wash and shampoo, then found a cheap motel that accepted cash. An hour later, after nearly scalding herself standing in a hot shower for as long as she could stand it, she crawled beneath the covers and finally gave in to her exhaustion. Blessed blackness overtook her for several hours. Hours in which she dreamed of Michael. Of being in his arms. Of feeling his strong calloused hands stroking her. Of his lips, his tongue, and his glowing green eyes.

It didn't matter that their last moments together hadn't ended well. That was the awesome thing about fantasies. You could keep the parts you liked and edit the ones you didn't.

No matter what, he would always be her first.

Probably her only.

The next day, she went into town and got the lay of the land to see if it was worth sticking around for a few weeks, maybe months. First on her list was getting a job and replenishing her cash. Second was finding a walk-in clinic where she could get her insulin. If those two panned out, then she'd look for a better place to stay.

Job pickings were slim, especially night shift positions. Thankfully, she found a job waitressing in a biker bar, with the option of dancing should she be so inclined. She was not.

Not for the first time, she thought about the fortune that was held in her name, and how she'd never have to worry about money again. All she had to do was resurface and claim it.

Not a chance.

Krennersville was a cozy little town tucked among green, rolling hills a few miles off the interstate. It was close enough to get away in a hurry, but far enough (and unimportant enough) to deter most travelers from making an unexpected detour there. It was nice, but it couldn't compare to Birch Falls.

Bailey, now reinvented as Riley, shook her head and tried to put those kinds of thoughts behind her. She wasn't in Birch Falls any more. This was her life.

Until it was time to move on again.

* * *

Michael

Michael pulled into the parking lot of the bar. There were lots of bikes there, which did nothing to improve his mood. He got some curious looks when he walked in, but no one was stupid enough to say anything. One didn't need to be a rocket scientist to see that he wasn't someone to screw around with.

He took in the scene. As an avid biker himself, he'd been to plenty like it. Lots of smoke, leather, and dim lights, with pole dancers sporting straps and strings and metal studs. His gaze went to the stage first.

Dancing in scantily-clad, provocative outfits seemed out of character for the Bailey he knew, but, as a few phone calls from Ian had proven, he could easily fill a book with what he didn't know about his *croie*. Nevertheless, Michael breathed a sigh of relief once he established that Bailey was not one of those on the stage and raised platforms throughout the place.

These last few weeks had been hell. He'd been zigzagging from state to state up and down the east coast based on Ian's intel, following bus routes, trying to anticipate where she would appear next. Sometimes he was right, sometimes he was wrong, but he was always a few steps behind.

Until now.

Bailey was *damn* good at getting lost, but there was never a question that he *would* find her. The last positive hit they'd had – from a security camera in an eastern Kentucky bus terminal – had been at least a week earlier. After checking out every possible outgoing bus, plane, and train with no success, both he and Ian agreed she was cooling her heels and staying put, at least for the time being.

With some cash and a lot of footwork, Michael confirmed that she was holing up in a small dive on the outskirts of Krennersville. Once he knew where she was, he began his preparations.

The last few weeks on the road had given him time to think and work out a plan. Bailey was his *croie* and he was not going to leave anything to chance this time. No other woman had gotten under his skin as she had, soothing away the restlessness and the angst. No other woman had consumed his thoughts, waking or otherwise. And he'd never, *ever* lost control before being with her, not under any circumstances.

The more he thought about it, the more he was convinced that Bailey had felt that connection as well, but either she hadn't recognized it for what it was or she was fighting it. He was betting on the latter. He'd seen the way her eyes lit up when she saw him. Had felt it keenly in her kiss and the way she melted against him.

And she had felt strongly enough to give him her most precious gift: herself.

Michael didn't believe for a minute that she would have done so for anything less than a true, soul-to-soul connection. His gut told him so, as did her actions, and everything that Ian had been able to discover.

All he had to do was show her. He would tell her, too, but words were cheap until she accepted the truth: that they were meant for each other. She was the only woman for him, and he the only man for her.

With that in mind, he'd gotten a suite at the closest swanky hotel, about thirty minutes down the interstate. Because once he found her, he was going to pamper and care for her, convince her that what he felt for her was more than industrial-grade animal lust.

He'd spent the last two hours checking out possible places of employment, primarily late night businesses that wouldn't ask a lot of questions. *Rumblers* was the last place within a two-mile walking radius. Part of him hoped she hadn't taken a job at the down and dirty club. Another part hoped she had, so he could get her the hell out of there and back in his arms again.

He took another look around the smoky interior. If she wasn't a dancer, then she had to be a waitress. Michael took one look at the skimpy outfits they were wearing and felt a bolt of white hot fire shoot through his body. Jean cut-offs that qualified more as high-cut panties, really, and skin tight T-shirts that displayed the name of the bar as well as a woman's entire midriff. He fought against the image forming in his mind of Bailey wearing that outfit. Of other men catching sight of that *luckenbooth* charm flashing in the lights…

He found a spot off to the side with a good view of the place and began scanning. Left. Center. Right. Center. Left. Back and forth his eyes moved, automatically assessing the patrons and the level of threat they posed, should it come to that.

A server passed about twenty feet in front of him with a small, circular tray in her hand, loaded with drinks. She had a figure just like Bailey's – very curvy, with ample breasts, lush hips, and a tiny waist. He felt himself stir and took a closer look.

It sure as hell didn't look like his woman.

This woman's hair was much shorter than Bailey's, falling to just below her shoulders. Straighter than Bailey's natural loose curls, but still wavy. The color was all wrong, too. Rather than Bailey's midnight tresses, it was a shiny chestnut, with dark stripes of deepest cherry peeking through.

The way she moved was very familiar, though. Not a single wasted motion, graceful, perfect balance. As she glided through the crowd from one table to another placing drinks in front of them, he recognized the hypnotic sway of her hips, the gentle curve of her thighs and calves. His dick went instantly hard. His eyes might be questioning her identity, but the rest of him wasn't.

Ian's words echoed in his head. *"Any distinguishing features? And I don't mean hair or eye color – those things are easily changeable."*

It was her, but her appearance had changed. Her new look was just teetering on wild, a far cry from the quiet, shy waitress that had served him coffee at his grandfather's diner. And unlike that cute little pink and white outfit she wore while working for his grandfather, this uniform left very little to the imagination.

Just looking at all those abundant feminine curves beneath the stretched fabric made him hard as steel, and he knew for certain he wasn't the only one. Any straight man would have to be either castrated or clinically dead not to feel the effects, but then, that was the whole idea, wasn't it? The fact that other men had been able to look at what was exclusively his made him crazy. He wanted to kill everyone who dared to look at her and burn the fucking place to the ground.

The intensity of his reaction surprised even him. He'd never had a problem with self-control before. Yet around this woman, everything went to shit. His brain stopped working and his primal instincts roared to life. Instincts that demanded he claim and protect her with every fiber of his being. He felt like the rational part of his brain was offline and the automatic, primitive response center in the brain stem had taken control.

One of the men at the table she was serving reached up to pat her ass, and a red haze colored Michael's vision. In two strides he was there, murder in his eyes.

"Keep your fucking hands off her."

The waitress froze at the sound of his voice. Michael placed himself between her and the man at the table, who was slowly rising to his feet, along with the other three men seated there.

Michael moved so fast it was hard to see. With one side-armed fist to the face, the guy to the right was suddenly sitting right back in his chair, eyes unfocused. One duck and two quick jabs later, the other two were down. The guy who had dared to put his hand on her ass backed up a step when Michael advanced. Quick as lightning, Michael's hand shot out and wrapped around the man's wrist. The man let out a sudden cry when the bones in his hand snapped under the pressure.

"You owe the lady an apology," Michael snarled.

"Sorry, sorry, sorry!" the man wheezed. "You broke my fucking hand!"

Michael punched him once in the face to shut him up, ignoring the splatter of blood that coated his knuckles. With a much gentler touch, he placed his hand around Bailey's upper arm and steered her toward the exit. "You are coming with me," he said, leaving no room for argument. Wide eyes – *hazel* eyes – blinked back at him.

Two overly large bouncers met them at the door.

"Problem, Riley?" one of them asked, shooting a look at Bailey.

"There's no problem," Michael told him. "We were just leaving."

"Not if the lady doesn't want to leave with you, you're not."

"It's okay, Tank," said a familiar voice, low and velvety, just as he remembered. "I'm done for the night anyway."

The one called Tank gave her a once over. "You sure, babe?" The bouncer had a soft spot for her; he could see it. Michael reined in the urge to put his fist right through it and relieve the man of several vertebrae.

* * *

Bailey

Bailey gave the bouncer a small smile and nodded. *Michael was here.* She didn't know how he found her, or why, exactly, but she did know she didn't want to cause any more of a scene. Fights were a common occurrence here, and if they left quietly now, they might be able to make it out before the rest of the Demon Spawn gang showed up and saw what Michael had just done to four of their members.

"Yeah, I'm good. Thanks."

Out in the cool air, Michael led her deeper into the parking lot. He walked quickly and she was forced to jog to keep up with the hold he had on her. After about twenty paces he stopped, pulled her into his arms and kissed her as if his very life depended on it. It was a deep, searing, desperate kiss, managing to capture everything she felt and give it right back.

Then, just as quickly, he was pulling her farther across the lot until they reached his truck.

"Riley? Is that what you're calling yourself now?" he asked, raking his gaze over her from head to toe.

It was a powerful gaze, sending burning heat everywhere it touched before turning away. He moved restlessly from one foot to the other, pacing back and forth in front of her, jaw clenched and green eyes aglow. He was trying hard to keep himself under control, she could sense that. Like a wire that had been stretched too tight for too long and was ready to snap. Even like this, her body craved his; her heart and soul screamed for his complete and undivided attention.

Bailey said nothing, unable to fully accept what was right before her eyes. She wrenched her gaze away and cast it down toward the pavement, her mind whirling frantically.

Michael was here. Michael had found her. Why?

He stopped pacing temporarily to glare at her again. "Love the hair, too. Looks a lot like Stacey's, as a matter of fact. The colors are more striking, I have to admit, but the effect is quite lovely."

Bailey remained quiet, knowing she didn't have the answers he wanted to hear. She kept a small distance between them, arms wrapped tightly around herself, her gaze on her shoes. Anger and something else – relief? - rolled off of him in waves. Exactly why he was so mad, she wasn't sure. But whatever the reason was, it was enough for him to track her down.

The chill of the November evening seeped into her weary bones, accelerated by the cold sweat breaking out all over her. She hugged herself tighter, but could not stop the full-body shudders that began to take hold.

Cursing, Michael removed his leather jacket and handed it to her. If she'd been stronger, she would have shoved it back into his chest, but she wasn't. In the haze of the bar, she'd been able to keep moving, and as long as she was moving, she was all right. It was when she stopped that she started having issues. Standing out in the cold in her minimal clothing, it was all catching up to her.

Her system was messed up due to repeated, lack of sleep and an unbalanced diet. Even her insulin injections had become irregular thanks to the strict identification requirements at the clinic. Since she couldn't produce anything to confirm she was who she said she was, they would only give her the injections there instead of giving her a prescription to do it herself. Since she couldn't get there twice a day during normal business hours, it was playing havoc with her system.

Not for the first time, Bailey cursed the digital age and the recent changes in the health care industry. She was diabetic. What the hell else did they have to know? Did it really matter what name she'd been born under?

Bailey wrapped herself inside his jacket, inhaling deeply. The scent of it made her head swim, but even the residual warmth of his body heat could not warm her. She pulled it tighter around her, covering as much of her body as possible, and waited.

* * *

Michael

Her complete lack of protest bothered Michael more than the yelling response he'd expected. The prickling on the back of his neck grew stronger. Something was wrong. He blew out a breath and took a closer look. Maybe in his jealousy-induced rage he'd made a mistake.

Her skin was pale, much lighter than the soft bronze he remembered. Her face was drawn, as if she hadn't eaten or slept in days. Even the considerable amount of makeup she wore wasn't enough to hide the dark circles beneath her eyes. Her *hazel* eyes, not the gorgeous swirling turquoise he remembered.

"It *is* you, isn't it, Bailey?"

Half of her face was tucked into the collar, forcing him to lean over to see her, but there was no mistaking the slight nod she gave him, or the subtle sniffle that suggested she was trying to hold back tears.

Michael was nearly beside himself. "Christ, Bailey. What the fuck is going on?"

He barely had time to catch her before she swayed and fainted.

Michael laid her out on the bench seat and covered her body with the thermal blanket he kept in the back. He felt her pulse. It was slow but strong. Lifting her eyelids, he spotted the contact lenses, removing them ever so carefully. He sucked in a breath when he discovered that one eye was remarkably blue, while the other was a clear emerald green.

After assuring himself she was in no immediate danger, he strapped her in the best he could and drove her to his hotel. He used the back entrance to ensure privacy—one of the perks of staying in the VIP suite—cradling her in his arms. She never even stirred.

Once in his suite, he swiftly removed her uniform and stuffed it into the trash. She'd never wear that again, that was for sure. He briefly considered burning it, then thought better of it when he spotted the sprinklers and smoke detectors in every room.

Laying her out on the king-size bed, he checked her over more thoroughly. No bruises, a few minor scratches, but nothing that would indicate abuse or drug use, forced or otherwise. He concluded that she was suffering from exhaustion and possible dehydration.

He used the finger stick kit he'd brought along with him and was shocked to find her sugar levels way off. Thankfully, his careful preparations had included stocking up on pre-measured insulin syringes, thanks to his doctor cousin, Michael Callaghan. After ripping open one of the packages he'd brought with him, he gave her an injection, then pulled the covers around her and held her tightly against him.

It was going to be a long night, but the important thing was, she was here in his arms, exactly where she belonged.

chapter thirteen

Bailey

Bailey was having a wonderful dream. She was tucked safely in Michael's arms, spooned against his hard, strong body. It was so realistic she swore she could feel his warmth and the beat of his heart against her back.

Something soft covered them, thick and luxurious against her bare skin. She didn't want to wake up. Instead, she held on to the dream, reveling in the fantasy. She knew she was hallucinating, probably because she was overdue for her injection again, but it was too good, too perfect, not to enjoy for just a little while longer.

When her hallucination started caressing her stomach, however, she knew she was on the verge of losing it completely. The granite shaft nestled snugly against her behind felt all too real. She tried to turn over, but iron arms held her in place.

"Shh. Go back to sleep," a deep, familiar voice

purred. *It couldn't be. Could it?*

"Michael?"

"Yes, I'm here. It's okay, Bailey. Rest."

As if. Bailey was suddenly aware she was only wearing a thin cotton t-shirt (probably his, given the loose comfortable fit) and a pair of panties. Her traitorous body responded to him instantly. Her breasts swelled and her nipples hardened; a rush of wet heat dampened those panties. She forced herself to recall what happened the last time she'd felt like this, and that helped temper her lust.

"What's going on?"

Michael loosened his grip enough to allow her to turn toward him, but not enough to break free. He propped his head up on one hand, keeping the other protectively just above her hip.

"You passed out in the parking lot of the bar and I brought you here. Do you remember?" His eyes searched her face.

Her mind rewound frantically; her heartbeat quickened into a racing gallop between one thump and the next. Images of him in *Rumblers*, taking out those bikers with astonishing ease. The sensation of his fragrant jacket surrounding her in the shadow of the parking lot. A warm, damp cloth brushed over her brow. Snippets of sipping something cool and delicious. They were dreamlike bits and pieces, disconnected and out of sequence.

"When?"

"About twenty-four hours ago."

"Twenty-four hours!" Panic welled in the pit of her stomach. After that long without insulin, she should be in shock or a coma, yet she felt strangely normal. "I need my purse."

"Relax, sweetheart. I've been giving you insulin injections every twelve hours. Your sugar levels have evened out."

She looked at him as if he'd grown two heads. "How could you possibly know?"

He was watching her closely. Too closely. Just what else had he been able to discover? Did he know who she was? How had he found her?

Her eyes raked across his bare shoulders and chest, down toward what was hidden underneath the sheet.

"I did nothing more than hold you, Bailey." His face darkened. "You had nightmares. Bad ones. The only thing that calmed you was when I held you." His green eyes smoldered. "I promise you, you will be wide awake when I make love to you again, and I'm going to show you just how pleasurable it can be."

She stiffened at his arrogant assumption, even as her core clenched in wanton hope. "There won't be a next time, Michael."

He gave this the briefest moment of thought. "Don't you think it will be difficult to share my bed every night and not make love?"

She gasped at his arrogance. "I will not be sharing your bed, so that shouldn't be a problem."

"Of course, you will. Where else would my wife sleep but in my bed?"

The man was certifiable. "You seem to be under the impression that I'm going to marry you."

"There is no doubt in my mind whatsoever that I'm going to marry you," he said confidently. "And, if you recall, I did tell you, so you can't say you weren't forewarned."

Imperious, presumptuous *impossible* man! Yet he *had* said he was going to marry her, hadn't he? That night at the diner, after he'd rescued her from Tommy's and before they'd gone up to the lake. But she'd thought he was joking, of course.

"I don't recall you asking."

"A mere technicality." He waved his hand impatiently. "One we can rectify right now." Michael eased from the bed with a masculine grace that belied his size. She was relieved (and slightly disappointed) to see that he was not, in fact, fully naked, but wore thin sweat pants.

Then he went down on bended knee and took her hand in his.

"Bailey Keehan, will you marry me?"

Her heart stuttered and stopped for several breaths before kicking in again. "No."

Michael grinned, not in the least bit daunted by her blatant refusal. "You love me."

Bailey broke eye contact. She couldn't deny it. Just as she could never look into his eyes and lie to him. His grin widened.

"You do! You love me."

* * *

Michael

Michael's heart soared. She might not be happy about it, but by not denying it, she had just admitted that she loved him. Of course she did. She was his *croie*.

"That's beside the point," she sniffed.

Bailey swung her legs over the side of the bed. He was there before her feet hit the floor. Her sugar levels might have evened out, but a full twenty-four hours in bed, occasionally sipping juice and broth, would make anyone weak and wobbly.

He wrapped his arms around her until she got her balance. So what if she didn't return the embrace? At least she wasn't pushing him away.

"Baby, that's *exactly* the point. We were made for each other. You feel it, too."

"You don't know anything about me," she shot back.

"I know enough," he countered. "I know you are the only woman I would ever chase up and down the east coast. The only woman who has ever managed to reach inside me and touch my soul. The woman I love, my soul mate, my perfect match. Everything else is irrelevant."

* * *

Bailey

He pulled her closer until her cheek lightly rested against his collarbone, and dipped his head so his lips brushed against her ear. She felt his warm breath against her skin, sending shudders of tingles through her core. Her inner muscles contracted in response to his breathy whisper, spoken with a lusty Irish lilt.

"Marry me, *leannán*."

Marry me, lover. Despite her best efforts to remain steadfast, Bailey's knees went weak and her head swam dizzily. Whether it was because of his nearness or his whispered words of love, she didn't know, but she was grateful for the strong arms that kept her from collapsing.

"Michael…"

Just that quickly, that fluttering feeling in her chest dropped into her stomach and became a full-blown roil. Her hand flew up to her mouth. A second later she shoved at him – hard – and sprinted toward what she hoped was the bathroom.

Without pretense, he held her hair and rubbed her back while she retched into the commode. When the worst of it was over, he handed her a cool, damp cloth. She couldn't help but think how she had done the same for his sister in what seemed like another lifetime.

For all intents and purposes, it *was* another lifetime. She was not the same person. Different name. Different look. Different life.

"Well, that's not quite the reaction I was hoping for."

Bailey gave him a weary smile.

"Thanks," she said, reaching for the cup of mouthwash he held out to her. It was cinnamon-flavored, her favorite. She should have been more surprised than she was.

"You had that in your back pack," Michael said as if guessing her thoughts. "I picked up your things from your motel room."

Before she could fully process that, he asked, "Does this happen often?"

His green eyes had darkened to emeralds and were filled with concern. It was hard to summon a defense when he looked so genuinely worried about her. It was hard to summon a defense against him, period. This man did things to her. Things she couldn't explain.

Bailey swished the red liquid around and then spat it out into the toilet, sidestepping his question with one of her own. "You always seem to catch me at my best, don't you?"

He gave her a wry smile. "I'll take it any way I can get it, sweetheart. How long have you been sick?"

Bailey exhaled slowly and attempted to stand up, then decided that wasn't happening yet and settled for putting the lid down and sitting on the toilet with her head between her knees. "I'm not sick, Michael."

"Then why ...?" Michael suddenly dropped to his knees and placed his hands on her shoulders. His voice was quiet, guarded. "Bailey, are you pregnant?"

Almost imperceptibly, her head nodded.

"You're carrying our child? We're going to have a baby?" Another nod. Before she could take her next breath, she was lifted off of her feet and crushed against his chest.

Michael laid her on the bed and proceeded to apply butterfly-light tender kisses across her face. She closed her eyes, welcoming the soothing darkness behind her lids. Michael disappeared for a moment, but when he came back, he began lifting the hem of the shirt she wore.

She stopped him by putting her hands over his. "What do you think you are doing?"

"Taking care of the mother of my child."

"Michael."

"Don't argue with me, Bailey. You're in no shape to fight me and you know it."

His voice was firm, almost commanding, a tone she'd heard him use on others but never her. She hesitated. A big part of her wanted to do exactly as he said and let him take control for a little while. She was tired, so very tired of trying to handle everything on her own.

"That's a good girl," he said approvingly when she stopped resisting. His tone was softer, soothing. When she was undressed, he lifted her into his arms. Then he lowered her into the oversized Jacuzzi tub, which he had somehow managed to fill with warm water and soothing bath scents. She couldn't help the moan of pleasure as the water surrounded her.

Michael proceeded to wash her hair, using the pads of those strong, skilled fingers to give her a scalp massage. Afterward, he gently rinsed her hair with cups of water, carefully avoiding her face. His touch was nothing less than magical, sending her protests into the background temporarily.

"You could work in a salon," she murmured dreamily. "Women would pay big bucks for this kind of treatment."

Michael chuckled. "I did, actually, when I was much younger. Thought it would be a great way to meet women. Plus the tips helped put me through my first year of college."

She couldn't help but smile, picturing a young, hot Michael Connelly surrounded by a roomful of women dying for him to put his hands on them. "And how did that work out for you?"

"Not so well, actually. You wouldn't believe what some of those women propositioned." He shook his head, looking properly scandalized. "And me, such an impressionable, innocent young lad. It was quite tragic, really. Scarred me for life."

A small laugh bubbled up through her. Bailey was unable to picture him ever being *that* innocent. "Are you telling me that you didn't take them up on their propositions?"

"I'll plead the fifth on that," he said with a devilish grin, invoking his constitutional right not to incriminate himself.

Bailey would have smacked him had she had the energy to do so. But that would have meant raising her arm out of the glorious bathwater and it just wasn't worth it.

Her hair now clean and fragrant, he gently towel-dried it, then wrapped it expertly in a towel.

"Now for the rest," he crooned.

Bailey held out her hand for the washcloth he'd just soaped up, but he pushed it away. "You will let me do this for you, Bailey."

"Why?" she asked softly.

"Because I need to."

The quiet sincerity in his tone and the plea in his eyes stilled any further objection. He proceeded to wash her reverently, his hands working magic everywhere he touched. It made her crave more but, somewhat disappointingly, it went no further.

When she was thoroughly cleansed, he reached into the large cylindrical white thing (which turned out to be a towel warmer) and extracted a fluffy white body towel. Helping her out of the tub, he wrapped it around her, cocooning her in soft warmth, then carried her back to the bedroom.

A girl could get used to this kind of pampering, she thought. Then realized the impossibility of such a thing.

Bailey closed her eyes and sank back into the pillows, feeling a warmth that did not come entirely from soaking in a hot bath. No one ever said life was fair, but this just seemed overly cruel. Why did God, or Fate, or whatever was in control of this effed-up planet keep reminding her what she couldn't have? She must have done something horrible in a previous life to screw up her karma this badly, because she sure couldn't think of anything she'd done in *this* lifetime to warrant it.

The bottom of the bed dipped under Michael's weight. The next thing she knew, he picked up one of her feet and began massaging it with both hands with heavenly strokes and squeezes that nearly had her purring in satisfaction. When he finished with one, he began with the other.

Cruel, cruel, cruel.

"Don't tell me you worked as a masseur as well?"

"All right, I won't." The smug grin on his face, not to mention the skill and strength of his hands, told her everything she needed to know. "But med school is expensive."

That was unexpected. "Med school? You're a doctor?"

"No. I started out that way, but found out soon enough I wasn't cut out for it."

Her jaw dropped. "What then?" She realized she had absolutely no idea what he did for a living.

"I enlisted in the Army. Became a Ranger." He spoke casually, as if it was no big deal. At least it explained the whole lethal aura thing he had going. And how he had been able to handle those bikers – and her stalker – so easily.

"But you're not anymore?"

"Once a Ranger, always a Ranger," he said with a tight smile. "But not an active one. When my last tour ended, I didn't re-up."

"What happened?"

Michael's face darkened. "It was getting too easy to kill. Sometimes I couldn't tell who the good guys were anymore. So I finished my tour and wandered around for a while, figuring out what I wanted to do. Eventually, I went back to Birch Falls. Reconnected with the family. Plus I wanted to open up a premiere fitness center in the area."

Michael's hands moved up to her calves, then her thighs as he spoke. They felt wonderful. With every place he touched, she melted a little more. He gently coaxed her onto her stomach, pulling the covers up just over her behind. Then he put those magical fingers to work on her back.

Her words were slightly muffled against the pillow. "You could patent those hands," she told him.

He chuckled softly. "My services are rather exclusive."

"Are they now?"

"Yes, there is only one client that I will attend to personally these days."

Her heart stuttered again. "Oh? And who might that be?"

"That's confidential. I take the privacy of my clients very seriously."

"Hmmph."

He had worked his way up to her shoulders. Bailey tried to turn over but he held her firmly in place.

"I'm not finished yet."

She had no choice but to surrender. By the time he'd reached her neck, her entire body felt like a soft, gooey mass.

"Feeling better?" he asked finally, pulling the covers up to her neck, then easing off the bed.

"So much better."

"Good. Take a nap. I'm going to make you something to eat."

Even the thought of food had her stomach roiling again. "No, no food, please. I don't think I can hold anything down just yet."

"Trust me," he said, tucking the covers around her and kissing her forehead.

Cruel. Why did he have to be so damn gentle and caring?

"Michael, you don't have to do this."

She saw the briefest flash of anger in his green eyes, but his expression stayed controlled. "Sleep now, Bailey. Pick a fight with me later." An instant later he was gone and she found herself alone.

She hated how cold she felt without him. How was she ever going to find the strength to walk away again?

chapter fourteen

Bailey

Despite her protests, Michael insisted she sip the broth he'd prepared in the small kitchenette, as well as nibble a few crackers. Surprisingly, the light meal stayed down and she felt better afterward. She didn't share that with him though. The sexy bastard was already looking quite pleased with himself without her encouragement.

After removing the tray he joined her in bed, fully clothed, and on top of the covers. He snatched up the remote and began flipping through the channels.

"What are you doing?"

"It's been a long day. Thought I'd lay in bed with my wife and watch some TV."

She huffed, a soft feminine sound that caused the left corner of his mouth to quirk slightly. "I'm not your wife. And I don't watch television."

"You will be," he said confidently. So

confidently that her heart skipped a beat. "And why don't you watch TV?"

She shrugged. It was difficult to explain to someone why each added utility was another breadcrumb she didn't need. Besides, given the bits and pieces she'd seen, she wasn't missing much. But he was looking at her, expecting an answer, so she said, "I'd rather read a book."

She could have sworn she saw a smirk ghosting over his lips, as if he somehow knew about her closet obsession with steamy romance novels. Then again, if his methods of tracking her down involved a stop at her Birch Falls apartment, he would have seen the stack of second-hand paperbacks that she'd acquired. Thankfully, though, he said nothing.

Apparently, Michael didn't find television any more interesting than she did. He clicked through about a hundred channels (at least it seemed that way) until he paused on a chopper show. Bailey did a double-take when she saw the familiar face filling the screen.

"Hey! It's Kyle," she said, sitting up. "Wow. He looks... *wow*." With his long black hair tied back, ever-present shades, and black leather, he looked seriously deadly.

"Bailey," Michael warned, "don't talk about another man when you're in bed with me. And I don't think my sister would appreciate you perving on her husband."

"I was not *perving* on him," she protested. "I

was thinking how different he looks on TV compared to the last time I saw him. On this show he seems like a real ... I don't know ... *badass*, I guess."

Michael snorted. "I've got news for you, sweetheart. Kyle *is* a badass."

"Funny, I didn't get that at all when I saw him at the ER that night. He was so gentle with Lina, and the look on his face – like she was his whole world."

"Yeah," Michael said softly. "That's what happens when a man finds the right woman, Bailey. She becomes his whole world, and he'll do anything for her."

Bailey had the distinct impression they weren't talking about Kyle anymore. She dropped her gaze and picked up another cracker to nibble on.

After surfing through at least a dozen more channels and not finding anything they could agree on, Michael snapped off the TV and began undressing, tossing his clothes over the back of a chair as he did.

"What are you doing now?" she asked as her eyes followed every ripple on each expanse of skin he revealed.

"I'm tired, and I'm going to bed."

"You're taking off all your clothes."

"Yeah. I sleep naked."

He slid under the covers, careful to keep space between them and gave her a pointed, challenging, panty-wetting look. "Is that a problem?"

Problem? No, there was no problem. Unless of course, she didn't *want* to have a gorgeous, sexy, tender, caring, confident man fully nude in bed with her and less than a foot away. She didn't want that, did she? Because if she did, she might just be tempted to move her hand a few inches, and then it would land right on his...

"You're ... aroused," she said, blinking rapidly as all the air in her immediate space seemed to vanish.

Michael glanced down, then gave her a sexy grin and a wink. "I'm always hard around you, sweetheart. Better get used to it."

Then the shameless rogue turned his back to her, punched his pillow once, and went to sleep, leaving her to stare at the back of those bare, broad shoulders and the sheeted contours of his fabulous ass. He must have known she was staring, too, because she distinctly heard him chuckle.

She grunted, then leaned over and sprinkled a few cracker crumbs on his side of the bed for good measure.

More than an hour later, Michael was breathing the deep, even breaths of slumber, but Bailey was still wide awake. How was she supposed to get any rest with him laying all gorgeous and naked next to her like that? Granted, according to him, she'd slept with him the night before, but that was different, because she hadn't *known*. Being wide-awake and completely aware was a whole new ballgame entirely.

He'd turned again. Now on his back, the sheets had somehow shifted lower and barely covered his hips (her restless shifting had nothing to do with that; it had just happened, somehow). To further exacerbate the situation, he was still very much aroused, judging by the nifty tent just over his groin. His arms were folded back under his head, as if he were contemplating the ceiling from beneath closed lids while showcasing his magnificent chest and exquisitely shaped biceps. Delicious heat radiated from him, too. Fragrant heat. Clean and spicy and male. She leaned over and inhaled deeply, filling her lungs with it.

Trying to maintain a safe distance between them was impossible. There was no such thing as a safe distance, not from him. If he was anywhere near her, her body behaved like a divining rod, bending in his general direction.

Little by little she inched toward him until the length of her body ran against his. He felt good – so warm and solid. *Surely a little snuggle wouldn't hurt, right?* Michael was out; he hadn't moved in ages. He'd never know.

With a deep sigh, Bailey finally relaxed. Within minutes, she was sound asleep.

Michael wrapped his arms around her and smiled into the darkness.

* * *

Michael

"Michael, we've got to talk about this."

He'd been waiting for it. Bailey picked at the toast and scrambled eggs he'd made for her, her brow creased with serious thoughts. He'd already eaten, having risen at the crack of dawn to shower and take care of some business. He was handling everything over the phone or via his laptop, which he'd set up on the desk in the living area of the suite.

"So talk."

When it appeared she wasn't going to eat anymore he removed her tray, then put his fingers against her inner wrist, taking her pulse. He counted silently, then nodded, pleased with the strong, steady rhythm.

He wiped her thigh with an alcohol wipe and gave her an insulin injection. At least she was no longer fighting him on that front; she'd even admitted he was quite good with a needle.

Small victories.

That completed, he looked up to find her watching him intently. He was mesmerized by the natural color of her eyes. One was incredibly blue, the other a clear emerald green, like his. Sometimes they were wary, sometimes bemused. This morning, they also held sadness.

He sensed it, too, like an approaching storm. She was gearing up for some bullshit about why she was fighting this thing between them. Since bringing her here, neither one of them had brought up why she'd left Birch Falls so suddenly, or her change in appearance, or any other aspect of the massive elephant in the room.

He wasn't going to let her go so easily, especially now that he knew she was carrying their child. If she didn't know that about him by now, she would soon.

When she opened her mouth several times but failed to speak, he took the lead. As she was his *croie*, so he was hers, and he was going to be there for her, no matter what. She wasn't alone anymore. Perhaps a gentle reminder/assurance was in order.

"Are you sleeping better?" he asked. Every night after she thought he was asleep she snuggled up to him and fell into a deep, sound slumber. It was the only time she allowed herself to get close to him. Her subconscious had accepted what her conscious self hadn't yet.

"Yes," she admitted with a sigh. "Michael, I don't know how to say this."

Here it comes. He mentally girded himself for what was sure to be a laundry list of excuses. "Just say it."

She took a deep breath, gathering her courage. "I appreciate everything you've done, but I don't need you hovering over me like this. I'm fine now, and perfectly capable of taking care of myself."

It was a pretty speech. And complete bullshit. "I disagree."

"I beg your pardon?"

"I disagree, Bailey. You're not fine. And as for taking care of yourself, you weren't eating properly, you weren't sleeping enough, and you weren't even taking your insulin regularly. Oh, and let's not forget that you were working your ass off in a smoke-filled bar catering to horny, drunken bikers. You're *pregnant*, Bailey. What the hell were you thinking?"

Bailey flinched back as if he'd slapped her. He'd intended to remain calm and rational, but once he got going, he found it hard to stop. The worry that had plagued him from the moment she took off until he saw her in the club finally overflowed in a torrent of angry words.

"Were you even going to tell me? It's one thing for you to turn tail and run away with no regard for me or anyone else who cares about you, but this is a *baby* we're talking about. *Our* baby, Bailey. And I'll be damned if you think you're going to keep me away from my child, no matter how much you despise me."

He clamped his jaw shut, got up and paced across the room, running his hand through his hair. *Way to stay in control*, he seethed. *As if she needs a reminder of what an asshole you can be.* But goddamn it, it had to be said, because he wasn't walking away. Not from her, not from their child.

Seconds ticked by, turning into minutes.

"I didn't begin to suspect I was pregnant until a few days before you found me," she finally said, her voice quiet. "So I went out and bought one of those tests at the drugstore. When it came out positive, I admit, I got scared. But I wouldn't do anything to hurt the baby. Not ever. The only reason I was even at the bar that night was to quit. They couldn't find a replacement that quick so I agreed to stay one last night, but that was it."

Her lip started to tremble. Her voice grew louder. "I can't help it if I haven't been able to keep food down. You think I like throwing up every time I try to eat something? It's awful!"

The tears began to flow in earnest, rolling unchecked down her face as her emotions rose to the forefront. "And I can't believe you think I despise you, you stupid bastard! I couldn't sleep because every time I close my eyes all I see is *you*. I want you so much it hurts."

The moment the words were out of her mouth, Michael's anger evaporated. *I want you so much it hurts,* that's what she'd said. And that's what he understood, more than anything else, because that described his situation perfectly. Now that they were both on the same page, they could actually do something about it.

He couldn't move fast enough to pull her into his arms. "Christ, Bailey. I'm so sorry, baby. I know

I fucked up."

She mumbled something into his chest, her words so muffled he couldn't understand what she was saying.

"What was that?" He held her away from him just far enough to be able to see her face, wiping away the tears with his thumbs.

She took a shuddering breath. "I'm sorry, too, Michael. I thought I was ready. I know I should have told you but I didn't because I wanted so much for you to be the one to... to be my first. I was afraid you might stop if you knew. But then it really *hurt* and I panicked. I shouldn't have taken off like that. I knew it was only a one-time thing going into it, but somewhere along the line I fell in love with you even though I knew better, and I couldn't bear to see the regret in your eyes. I had to get away before I humiliated myself even more."

His heart swelled, though it was clear she hadn't realized what she'd admitted in her rush of words. "Say that again."

Bailey sniffled and blinked, her expression defeated. "I humiliated myself?"

"No, before that."

"I had to get away?"

"Before that."

She blinked again. "I fell in love with you?"

"That." *Finally.*

* * *

Bailey

She hadn't meant to say those words to him, not now, not ever. But before she could attempt to repair the damage, Michael leaned down and fit his mouth against hers. It started off like the others — axis-tilting — but then ratcheted straight up to "alternate universe" level. It was as though she could feel him pouring his heart and soul into her through that kiss. While her head swam, her body re-enacted her fifth-grade science "states of matter" experiment, going from solid to liquid to vapor and in less time than that ice cube had above the Bunsen burner.

By the time he pulled away, she didn't know what state she was in. Nor did she care.

"I love you, too, baby." He brushed her tears away with a feather-light brush of his thumbs. "And once I was inside you, I completely lost my mind. If I'd been remotely sane, I'd have realized it was your first time and I would have done things differently. When I realized what I'd done... God, Bailey. That wasn't pity you saw in my eyes, that was disgust with myself for hurting you and being such a selfish bastard."

She sniffled. "It was?"

He nodded. "Being with you was the best thing I ever felt, because you are the one for me, baby. My heart. My *croie*."

"I am?"

Another nod, a flex of strong fingers at the small of her back. "I think I suspected it from the first time I saw you at the diner, but I didn't know for sure until you ran into my arms that night at Tommy's."

"You did?"

Bailey felt a twinge of hope beginning to rise in her heart. He cupped her face with his hands. "And I have been dying to make it up to you. To show you just how good it can be." Planting tender kisses over her face, he murmured, "I want to make love to you, Bailey. Right here. Right now. Please."

She shivered beneath the intensity of that declaration. Her traitorous body tingled, wanted nothing more, but she hesitated. She'd been caught up in the maelstrom of desire for him before, and that hadn't ended well. But they were being given a second chance. And he knew the truth now, right? It would be better this time.

"We'll go slowly? You'll be patient with me?"

"Yes, I promise. I need you, Bailey. Being without you is just not an option. I would do anything for you."

Michael kissed her, at first a gentle, tender kiss that quickly deepened into something much more. He pulled at her bottom lip lightly until she opened for him and let him in. Between one breath and the next, his tongue swept skillfully across her lips and then dipped into her, tasting her. He groaned, coaxing her into returning his kiss.

What the man could do to her with a kiss!

Breaking away from her mouth, Michael lavished hot, wet kisses beneath her jaw, and down her neck, focusing on her pulse points. Everywhere he touched instantly became his; there was no use fighting it. He had already won.

She tilted her head back into the pillow to give him better access, running her hands through his thick, silky hair. Before long he was moving south again, licking along her collarbone, then blowing softly over her moistened skin and giving her shivers and concentrated bursts of tingles in her most sensitive areas.

He paused at her breasts, breathing heavily, his eyes filled with such hunger. She half-expected (*wanted*) him to stop and ravish them a little (*a lot*), but kept his promise, his touch light and reverent. He cupped them in his hands, massaging gently as his tongue created a path downward with agonizing slowness. Warmth flooded between her thighs, and Bailey felt the accompanying ache in her breasts, swollen and begging for more of his attention.

Michael's tongue traced around one nipple; his hot breath created the most wonderful sensations as he blew across them. She cried out when he finally sucked the hard tip into his mouth, nipping her lightly, then soothing the bite with his hot tongue. He continued rubbing, sucking, licking and biting for an eternity, alternating from one breast to the other, until she was nearly sobbing with need.

Leaving her nipples swollen and ultra-sensitive, Michael moved down over her belly, kissing each and every inch. "I'm going to spend hours here," he whispered against her skin. "Caressing you. Kissing you. Talking to our child. I'm going to show you just how good it can be, Bailey. So good you'll never doubt me again."

She arched and cradled his head, his words washing away the last remaining vestiges of doubt. And then he was moving again, taking his attention down to her legs. With long, slow licks and tiny, stinging bites he worked his way from the tops of her thighs to the inside, opening her to him, with hands that seemed to be everywhere at once – on her hips, then along her thighs, then behind her knees.

When he finally touched her *there*, she nearly screamed. He ran his finger gently up and down her soaked folds, humming his approval. She answered by tangling her fingers into his hair and tugging.

"So eager," he chuckled. "But not eager enough."

He positioned her legs over his broad shoulders, giving him unimpeded access. When he replaced his finger with his tongue, her eyes rolled back in bliss. So skillful was he with his onslaught, she gave up trying to fight it and let it — let him — take her any way he wished, until she couldn't stand another second.

"*Michael!*"

Lips and tongue swirled and sucked while his fingers penetrated and curled deep. Her entire body tightened; she gasped for breath. With her fingers clutched at his head, she tilted her hips, bracing for the orgasm that would shatter her. Every muscle tensed until she snapped, releasing wildly around him, crying out his name.

And still he stroked, sucked, and licked, extending the climax until she begged for mercy.

He was her anchor, the only thing that kept her from breaking into a thousand pieces and floating off into space. Slowly, tenderly, he kissed his way back up her body until he lay beside her. Then he pulled her into his arms and held her.

"Oh, Michael," she breathed, once she had regained the ability to speak. "That was…"

"Good?" he murmured.

"Incredible. Intense. Amazing." Her arms wrapped around his neck and her body clung to his, unwilling to relinquish the skin-to-skin contact.

"Ah, baby, I'm just getting started." He kissed the corners of her mouth. Big hands caressed the curve of her back, then cupped her backside in a firm, possessive hold, drawing her against him. She draped her leg over his, only to feel the hot, hard length of him against her inner thigh. A ghostly echo of remembered pain cut into her orgasmic buzz.

"Relax, love. I won't hurt you," he promised

when her concern slipped over her lips.

She believed him.

Before long Michael's skilled hands and teasing mouth had her stirring again. Feeling his hard body fitted so perfectly against hers, it was impossible not to be aroused. She hadn't even realized she'd been rubbing her hips against him, but oh, how she ached for him. Ached for him deep inside.

The throbbing between her legs grew as her body prepared itself for him. In less time than she would have thought possible, she was fully prepared to beg. He continued to play with her until she could bear it no longer.

"Please, Michael, I want you inside of me," she crooned in his ear. His answer was a groan deep in his throat, guiding her hips as they rocked against him. "*Please*, Michael. Take me. Now, *please*."

"No." His answer was soft but firm as his mouth continued to make love with hers, his tongue doing all sorts of wicked things.

"Please, Michael. If you're trying to punish me, it's working. Now you're just being cruel."

She reached between them and grabbed his shaft, squeezed and stroked in an attempt to persuade him, while imagining it was another part of her clenched around him.

Michael placed both hands on her hips, lifting her easily as he slid beneath her, resting her on his pulsing cock. "I'm not going to take you, because *you* are going to take *me*."

Michael guided her until her hips hovered above his. Grabbing the base of his shaft, he held it for her.

Bailey licked her lips and looked into his eyes — his glowing, lust-crazed eyes — and realized what he was giving her. She felt him shaking beneath her, saw the need etched in his face and his tensed body, and felt a surge of power she'd never felt before. With a seductive smile that made him groan, she began to ease herself onto him.

His fingers gripped her hips like a vise, but his only movement was to roll his hips to improve the angle of entry.

"That's it, baby," he breathed. "Slow and easy. It's all you. Take what you need."

His voice broke off in a hiss as she dropped another inch. A stream of Gaelic oaths crossed his lips in a tormented whisper; she recognized them for what they were — a prayer for the strength to withstand her torture.

Knowing she could drive him to such a plea inflamed her further. She had all the power. She was doing this to him. This was another chance to love him, and it was the only chance she would need.

Her hands splayed across his chest, nails raking across his nipples. He cursed again and his hips bucked, but she was ready for it. She was learning to read him, to anticipate his responses, reveling in the control she had over him. He was hers.

The realization slammed into her like a bus. *He had given himself to her.* A tigress roared to life inside her, and her nails bit into his skin like claws. *She* was the one he wanted. *She* was the one he loved.

There was no pain this time as her sheath stretched around him, only an intense sense of fullness. Of completeness. She took another inch, circling her hips to ease his passage.

"Ah, Bailey, it's so good, baby. You're killing me with that tight, sweet pussy. I never thought death could be so fucking good."

Another inch, then two. He groaned. She watched him, fascinated, awed that she held the power to do this to him.

Bailey discovered that if she lifted a bit first, she could take more of him each time she lowered. Each mini-withdrawal allowed her to take him deeper, increasing her pleasure — and his, if the tortured look in his glowing eyes was anything to go by. She tightened around him every time she rose, then relaxed and took him deeper with each descent. Her slow, explorative pace had them both gasping for air.

"Sweet fucking hell, Bailey, I feel like I'm going to explode. I can't hold it much longer, baby."

The thought of Michael releasing deep inside sparked another rush of slick wet heat, allowing her to slide the rest of the way and take all of him. Now that there was no pain, she could appreciate the pulse of every throbbing vein, and knew that she would feel his release as if it was her own.

And she wanted it, wanted to feel his pleasure more than she'd wanted her own.

She squeezed her inner muscles, increasing the friction as she began a slow ride. Michael's hips joined hers, rolling in perfect synchronization. Bailey threw back her head, her skin slick with perspiration. She rode him faster, harder. The pressure continued to build until she was desperate for release, the sound of her flesh hitting his like a beautiful symphony when paired with her cries and his growls.

She took him. All of him. Held him inside her as they moved together, as sweet and perfect as any romantic fantasy she'd ever read about. Better, because it was *real*.

Her climax came barreling down, thundering as hard and fast as her heart. Beneath her, Michael's body tensed, letting her know that he was right there with her. And then they were there, falling together. Even as the first waves began to crash over her, she felt him begin to pulse inside her. As her inner muscles bore down hard, they grew hot with the sensation of his release. Each pulse took her farther, until there was nothing except the feel of scorching heat and incredible fullness surrounded by melting, shaking flesh.

It was even better than she'd imagined.

Bailey collapsed onto his chest, exhausted, and his arms were immediately around her, holding her close. She could feel his heart pounding in rhythm with hers, felt his breaths as if they were her own. She knew then with absolute certainty that no matter what, her heart belonged to him.

chapter fifteen

Michael

Bailey's eyes popped open when Michael tried to extricate himself from her full-bodied hold. Chest to chest, one of her arms lay beneath his neck, the other tucked around his waist. Her top leg was hooked behind his knee.

A low rumbling sound came from her chest and she tightened her grasp.

"Did you just growl at me?" Michael asked. She repeated the sound, making him laugh.

"It's time for your injection," he told her softly, kissing her cheek.

"I think you've injected me pretty thoroughly," she murmured against his throat before she kissed him there, following up with a languorous lick for good measure.

"I've dreamed of you doing that," he murmured, exposing his throat to give her better access.

"Oh yeah? What else have you dreamed of?" Her hand reached down toward his fast-growing erection, skimming over his abs. As much as he wanted to take her again, he promised himself after their second hot and heavy session that he'd give her time to rest and recover.

He caught her wrists and shoved his hips back, out of her reach. "I'll tell you if you promise to let me give you your insulin like a good girl."

She pouted, and his heart swelled. Then her eyes took on a mysterious twinkle. "One fantasy for each shot, that's the deal."

He appeared to consider this as he unwrapped the pre-packaged syringe. Her eyes dropped to his package and she licked her lips. A fiery bolt of lust surged as he imagined those lips around him, loving him with the same passion she'd exhibited the night before when she'd ridden him to climax. Keeping his promise to take things slow and gentle was going to be even more difficult than he'd thought.

When he sat on the edge of the bed, she tried to crawl into his lap. In a split second he flipped her onto her stomach. One hand landed a warning slap on her ass.

"Be a good girl or I will spank you," he said firmly.

"Is that a promise or a threat?" she asked. His cock throbbed when he saw the flash of heat in her eyes.

Note to self: gentle spanking might be more of

an incentive than a threat.

Michael gave her the injection, then put the used needle in the disposable sharps container on the nightstand. The fire in his eyes was unmistakable. His palm came up and landed another slap on her other cheek. A quick check with his fingers confirmed what he already suspected. She was every bit as turned on as he was.

Turning her over, he promised himself he'd do better next time and covered her body with his own. Her legs parted eagerly as he slid into her. "That, baby, is a promise."

* * *

Michael

"Just where do you think you're going?" Michael asked, reaching out to pull her back against him. Other than necessary trips to the bathroom and kitchen, they'd spent most of the last twenty-four hours in bed. Neither one of them was complaining.

"I'm hungry."

"You ate less than two hours ago."

In the past few days, Bailey had gone from barely being able to stomach broth to wolfing down everything he put in front of her. He took that as a good sign. She was already looking much healthier, the sickly pallor all but gone, and the fullness of her curves growing lusher every day. Despite the initial sickness, which he now believed had been mostly due to stress and poor self-care, pregnancy agreed with her. She was glowing, and he couldn't keep his hands off of her.

"I know," she sighed, snuggling into him. "But you're the one who knocked me up. It's a little late to start complaining now."

Michael's hand slid down to her belly protectively. It made him the happiest man in the world to know that she carried his child. Well, almost the happiest.

"Speaking of which, we still have the problem of you not agreeing to marry me yet." He felt her tense. The last few days had been pure bliss; neither of them had brought up the issue of marriage.

"Why won't you say yes, Bailey?"

Bailey rolled away from him and got out of bed. "It's not that easy. There are things you don't know. Things you don't understand."

"Then tell me, because I'm dying here."

He waited, resisting the urge to pull her back to him.

"I love you, Michael. Spending the rest of my life with you would be like having every fantasy I've ever had come true."

That sounded about right. "Then I don't understand what the problem is."

"You don't know who I am, Michael. You can't marry Bailey Keehan, because Bailey Keehan isn't a real person. Well, maybe there is a Bailey

Keehan somewhere, but it's not me."

Michael had already figured that much out a long time ago. He shrugged. "So? I'm in love with the woman, not her name. What difference does it make?"

She looked at him with something like pity and said softly, "It makes all the difference in the world."

He started to say something, but she held up her hand. She walked slowly over to the bed, then placed one knee on it and cupped his face. She kissed him long, and slow, and his heart rebelled. It felt too much like a goodbye kiss.

"Get dressed," she told him, moving away. "I cannot discuss this knowing you're all gorgeous and naked beneath that sheet. And you need to hear this."

Bailey grabbed some of the clothes Michael had picked up for her and disappeared into the bathroom. He slung on his jeans and a flannel shirt. When Bailey re-emerged, she was fully clothed in a soft pink t-shirt and jeans. The first thing she did was cross the room and button his shirt.

"Honestly, Michael. I can't think straight when I can see your bare chest like that."

His lips twitched, and he grabbed her hands in his, pulling them to his mouth for a kiss.

"And we can't talk about this in here, either," she said, indicating the bedroom. She tugged gently to get him to follow her into the next room.

"You sit here," she said, guiding him to the couch. Bailey quickly moved out of his arms' reach, hugging herself instead.

"Bailey, what the hell is going on?"

"Be patient with me, Michael. This isn't easy for me."

"I'm not going anywhere."

"You might change your mind when you hear what I have to say."

He shook his head. "Nothing you say can change how I feel about you."

Her features twisted for a moment as if in pain before she smoothed them out and took a deep breath.

* * *

Bailey

Bailey had hoped she would never have to have this conversation with him, but Michael deserved — and needed — to know the truth, because it now affected him as well.

"My name is not Bailey Keehan. Nor is it Riley Kirkpatrick, or Erin O'Shea, or any of the other dozen or so names I've been calling myself for the past ten years." She chanced a quick glance at Michael, but his face gave nothing away.

She bit her thumbnail, summoning the courage to continue. "I've been running, Michael. Running since I was fifteen years old. Only now I'm pregnant, and it's not going to be as easy to run anymore." She turned to Michael. "You have to promise me right now that if anything happens to me you will take care of our baby."

"*We* will take care of our child *together*. I won't let anything happen to you." There was steel in his eyes.

"Swear it to me, Michael. You're a good man. I need your word."

He nodded. Bailey relaxed slightly, breathing out a small sigh of relief. Without realizing it, her hand went protectively to her stomach. "Good."

She paced back and forth, trying to organize her thoughts. She'd thought about this moment a thousand times over the last few months, hoping it would never come.

"I told you my mother was Irish and my father was Scottish, yes?" Michael nodded.

"My mother was Irish, but her family had been in America for several generations. Most of them lived in the northeast. The men worked as coal miners, mostly. They were hard-working, blue-collar through and through. Good people."

"My father's family was about as far removed from that as they could get. They lived in Scotland, part of the upper echelon of society. Royal lineage, pure aristocratic bloodlines, the whole nine yards. My father, the eldest child and only son, was being groomed to take over the family business, as it were. He met my mother on a business trip to the States." She smiled ruefully at the irony of it. "She was a waitress in a little out of the way café. It was love at first sight."

"Anyway, neither family was accepting of the match. Both sides felt my mom and dad were making a huge mistake, and did everything they could to keep them apart. But in the end, true love prevailed and they eloped, turning their backs on their families and starting a new life together."

"They had me right away. Mom had always intended to go back to work, but they ended up having one baby after another." She smiled again. "Even after several years of marriage, they couldn't keep their hands off of each other. Fortunately, Dad was a smart man and a good provider. We weren't rich, but we were happy."

Bailey's face darkened. "But Dad's family wasn't content to leave things alone, especially when his father's health began to fail. By long standing tradition, everything was passed to the eldest male child. They pleaded with him to return to Scotland and assume his responsibilities for the family business, but he refused, saying he would only do so on the condition that they accept my mother and all of us as blood family."

"Finally, they gave in, but they weren't happy about it. From what I understand, my grandfather had come around, but my grandmother was mortified that my father had 'dirtied the bloodline' so to speak. She made no secret of the fact that she thought my mother was only interested in my father for their fortune, and we kids were nothing but the shameful result of her throwing herself at him. For my grandfather's sake, though, she curbed her tongue enough to convince my father that she would behave, and eventually he gave in."

"My dad's cousin, Simon, came to the States to work out the details. Simon had taken over a lot of my father's responsibilities when he left and was practically running the company. Dad was smart enough to want everything legalized so that if anything happened to him, the rest of us would be cared for as legitimate heirs. Mom was still skeptical; she said her instincts told her something awful would happen, but Dad said he had faith there was some good in his family."

"Unfortunately, Mom's instincts were right. Dad underestimated the greed and pride of his family, especially Simon, and the lengths they were willing to go to. Shortly after the papers were signed and filed at the lawyer's office, Simon talked Dad into going out to celebrate. That night, while Dad was away, there was a fire at our house."

Bailey's voice grew softer. She looked across the room at something only she could see. "We were all sleeping; it was late. I remember waking up because someone was shouting. There was so much smoke it was hard to see. My two younger sisters were in bed with me; the three of us managed to get out. I tried to go back for the others, but a fireman grabbed me and locked me and my sisters in a police car. Dad got there shortly after. He ran in to save mom and my brothers, but ... but they didn't come out."

Bailey suddenly found herself in Michael's arms. He held her close to him. She soaked up his warmth and strength. It took a few minutes for her to gather the strength to continue.

"I saw Simon that night, watching from a safe distance. He caught me looking at him from the police car. I will never forget the look on his face, Michael. Never. I knew then that he was behind everything. Maybe he hadn't lit the flame, but it was his doing. His and my grandmother's."

"The problem was, there was no proof. The fire marshal said the cause was most likely faulty wiring, but there was nothing wrong with the wiring in that house, nothing. Simon set it all up somehow. With my dad and my mom out of the way, he cleared a major obstacle in securing the future of the company. After the official ruling came out, I knew I had to disappear. I've been running ever since."

"Because you are the eldest child," Michael said.

"Yes." Bailey took a deep breath. "The lawyer handling the contracts was an old friend of my maternal grandfather's. Without Simon knowing, my father had a last minute clause put into the contracts. In the event anything happened to him, his eldest *child* — not his eldest *son* — was to gain control of the estate. Simon never expected that."

"You think Simon wants to kill you?"

"No. If something happens to me, everything goes to my sisters. If something happens to *them*, ownership of the company passes to the board since my father has no surviving siblings."

"Then why do you think he is looking for you?"

"Right after the funeral, Simon cornered me. The bastard didn't even have the decency to pretend like he gave a damn. He told me, in no uncertain terms, that he would make sure all of Dad's assets got tied up in probate, and I'd be left out in the cold with no way to care for my sisters. He had a solution, though. He said if I married him, he would allow my sisters to live with us and they would be well cared for."

"He figured if he married you, he'd get the company."

"In a manner of speaking. Tradition says that the ownership passes to the eldest *male* relative. As a daughter, I am, in effect, only a caretaker. By myself, I mean nothing to Simon. But my *son* would control everything."

Michael felt rage burn through him. "The son of a bitch."

"Exactly. I told Simon there was no way I would marry him, but he laughed and told me that it didn't matter. If he could get a child on me — with or without my acceptance of his proposal, or my cooperation, for that matter — he would get what he wanted. He could arrange for a fake wedding certificate easy enough. A paternity test would prove him the father. He'd have me declared unfit by someone on his payroll, take my son, and control everything."

"I'll fucking kill him."

"I wish it were that easy, Michael. Simon is an incredibly powerful man, with friends in very high places. He'll stop at nothing to get what he wants. As long as I remain missing, everything continues as is and Simon can't do anything about it."

"You've been on the run for a long time." She nodded in affirmation. "Why didn't Simon have you declared legally dead?"

"He could," Bailey confirmed, "but that's not going to get him what he wants. Upon my death, control passes to my twin sisters. Both would have an equal share, and at the most, Simon could only hope for half. He wants it all. Now that I'm pregnant – especially if our baby is a boy – that changes everything. My son will inherit everything."

Michael was quiet for a moment. "Forgive me if I'm wrong, Bailey, but if you marry me, wouldn't that solve all of your problems?"

Bailey rubbed her belly protectively. "As long as Simon's out there, you — and our child — will never be safe. He's plotted once to get what he wants and proven that he's not above taking a life."

"I can handle Simon. Leave it to me."

She sighed. "It's more than just Simon, Michael. Do you know what my husband would be subjected to?"

"I have a pretty good idea."

"I don't think you do."

Bailey stood up and faced him. She looked deep into his eyes and took a deep breath. Holding out her right hand, she said, "Pleased to meet you, Michael Connelly. I'm Keely McRae."

Other than a slight raise of an eyebrow, Michael's expression remained unaffected. "Keely McRae? *The* Keely McRae? The missing McRae Security heiress?"

Keely sank down into the nearest chair, suddenly exhausted. "Aye."

"I remember that case. Got huge media attention. Missing billionaire heiress, sobbing older fiancé with his face all over the news."

"Simon," Keely confirmed.

"A fucking media circus."

"Yeah, that pretty much sums it up. I'm so sorry, Michael."

"Don't be. It's not your fault, and it doesn't change the fact that I'm in love with you."

She gave him a weak smile. "I know that too." She had a lot of baggage. It wasn't fair to him or anyone else. One way or another, this had to stop.

Now she had a baby to think of. Michael's baby.

What was she going to do without him? She'd admitted that she loved him. She'd left him once and barely survived it. How was she ever going to do it again?

She swiped angrily at the tears that threatened to spill. She would not do this again. Not here. Not now. Damn Simon!

Michael pulled her into his arms, and instantly she began to feel better. He was so strong, and warm, and so ... *not shocked*. She placed both hands on his chest and pushed far enough away to look into his face.

"You already knew, didn't you?"

"Most of it, yes, but you filled in a few of the missing pieces."

"How?"

He grinned. "Remind me to introduce you to my cousin Ian sometime. But only after you've got my ring on your finger."

She didn't know whether to kiss him or slap him. At that moment, slapping him seemed like the better option.

"How could you let me go on like that?"

Michael looked straight into her eyes. "Because it had to be your decision to tell me. I don't give a shit who you are or where you came from. I've loved you from the first moment I laid eyes on you, before I knew your name, or any other thing that doesn't make a damn bit of difference to me, to us."

Bailey opened her mouth, but he didn't give her a chance to speak. "And before you say anything, I really don't give a shit about your money, either. Give it all to your sisters. I've got more than enough of my own to keep us comfortable for the rest of our lives."

She didn't know what to say. Michael Connelly had to be the best thing that ever happened to her.

"I only ask one thing," he said. She looked at him, wiping away the tears.

"What?" She would deny him nothing.

"Let me take care of Simon. My way." Michael's eyes glowed, and Bailey had never been so happy to have such a lethal man by her side. She nodded. "What will you do?"

A huge grin spread over his face. It was at once beautiful and terrifying. "Just leave it to me. Now," he said, standing up with her in his arms. "Marry me?"

"That's two things," she said, sniffling as she tried to wrap her mind around everything that had just happened. "You said only one."

"Ah, so I did." He held her firmly with one arm easily supporting all of her weight while the other proceeded to undo the fastening of her jeans. He expertly removed them single handedly, then pushed down his own pants until his erection sprang forth. He coaxed her legs around his waist and eased her down onto his shaft.

"What do you think you're doing?" she asked,

breathless.

"Making love to my wife," he murmured in between kisses along her neck.

"I'm not your wife."

"Maybe not on paper yet," Michael countered, "but you are in all the ways that matter. If you insist on our child being born out of wedlock, well…" He stroked in and out, erasing any retort that might have been forthcoming. "Though it will break my grandfather's heart, you know. He really likes you."

Bailey threw back her head, her hands grasping Michael's broad shoulders as he lifted her up and down the length of his shaft. "You don't play fair," she moaned.

"Never said I did." He pulled her down hard, filling her to capacity and hitting her sweet spot as she came powerfully around him, following only a second or two later. He sank back into the chair, keeping her sheathed around him as he cradled her body.

"You can be quite the caveman."

He was unapologetic. "When it comes to you, yes."

She snuggled against him, knowing his blatant admission should chafe against her female pride, but oddly enough, didn't. In fact, she had never felt more loved or cherished. That's how it would always be with him, she realized. A constant battle of wills with her dark knight, this man who still carried the dominant strains of his ancient Celtic warrior ancestors in his DNA.

She couldn't imagine anything she wanted more.

"Yes," she said finally.

"Yes?"

"Yes."

"Yes, what?" The corners of his lips tilted up, his green eyes dancing with triumph. She tried to pull away from him but he held her firmly with his hands on her hips. "Oh no you don't," he told her. "I want to hear it. All of it. From your lips. Willingly spoken."

Bailey effected a deep sigh, but her eyes were sparkling. "Michael Connelly, you are the most wonderful man in the world, my *croie*, and I am hopelessly and eternally in love with you." Her voice softened. "And there is nothing I want more than to be your wife and have your children. To fall asleep every night and wake up every morning in your arms. To spend the rest of my life by your side, no matter what. If you will have me."

* * *

Michael

Michael stared at her, speechless. He swore his heart would burst through his chest at any moment. Assuming it started beating again.

She looked into his eyes, a smirk dancing at the

corners of that very kissable mouth. "How's that?"
"That'll do," he whispered. "That'll do."

chapter sixteen

Bailey/Keely

St. Andrew's church in Birch Falls was standing room only when Michael Seamus Connelly and Keely Liadan McRae took their vows. Conlan gave the bride away. Kyle and Johnny served as the groomsmen. Celina and Stacey, both now glowing with the radiance of their pregnancies, were her bridesmaids. Keely's younger sisters, attending college in France, were unable to attend, but sent their best wishes along with a promise to visit on their next break.

Those strapping Irish lads from Tommy's made sure the media remained outside for the duration of the ceremony. The reception was to be closed as well, but as the bride and groom made their way to the limo, they were accosted by the press.

"You'd think they'd never seen a missing heiress get married before," Johnny muttered out of the side of his mouth. Michael smiled. He was taking it all in stride. At least until Simon MacKenzie appeared, waving legal papers and demanding media attention. The man was a consummate manipulator.

"This marriage is bogus!" Simon declared emphatically, once he was sure all cameras were on him.

"Why is that?" someone shouted, shoving a microphone into his face.

"Because Keely McRae is already married," he said, shocking the crowd into momentary silence. "To me." He proceeded to hand out copies of seemingly official documents to anyone who wanted one. Keely felt the blood begin to boil in her veins as Michael's hand tightened almost imperceptibly around her waist.

"Wait for it," he whispered.

"Keely, is that true?" Reporters flocked to her, her bodyguards forced to form a tight circle around the wedding party.

"Of course not," she said, holding her head high. Her voice was strong and clear, holding more confidence than she felt. As far as they knew, Simon was the grieving fiancé, his only crime being that he fell in love with a cold-hearted, calculating bitch who disappeared when she ripped out his heart. "Simon and I were never engaged, despite the lies he's been feeding you."

Simon looked properly shocked. "You deny that you carry my child?"

Keely gasped. How Simon had discovered her pregnancy she didn't know, but one look at the suspiciously satisfied look in her new husband's eyes was a big clue. She'd deal with him later.

"Of course, I deny it, you thieving, lying,—" Michael carefully pulled Keely back toward him, warning her with a discreet squeeze.

Simon faced the sea of reporters, appearing every bit the wronged soul. He looked over at the newlyweds, expecting to see panic, but instead, he saw was Michael, grinning from ear to ear. Keely thought he'd lost his mind. Out of the side of his mouth, Michael muttered, "Do you trust me?"

"Implicitly," she replied, equally quietly.

A moment later, police cars cruised into the street outside the church, along with black sedans containing no less than a dozen federal agents. For the first time, Simon's confidence faltered.

"Simon MacKenzie, you are under arrest for murder, embezzlement, forgery, and multiple attempts to bribe government officials."

Cameras flashed wildly as they placed him in handcuffs. His face turned a nasty purple color. Questions were fired at the agents and policemen alike, but all they received was the standard "no comment". Simon was taken away, his eyes murderous as he looked back at Michael, who continued to smile happily at him. From Michael's right, Ian gave a hearty wave followed by a thumbs-up.

Media attention whiplashed back to the couple. Michael sobered and held up his hand. Amazingly, the crowd quieted for him. His deep, resonant voice rang out clearly. "Simon MacKenzie has terrorized Keely McRae since she was a child. Now she can begin her new life. With me."

In front of God, guests, and national television cameras and crews, Michael took his new bride into his arms and kissed her so thoroughly that several women in the crowd nearly fainted.

Then he scooped her into his arms and carried her to the limo, flanked on either side by the rest of the wedding party, including seven bodyguards that looked remarkably like the groom, except for their brilliant blue eyes.

* * *

Bailey/Keely

Keely sat in her husband's lap, sipping the lemonade he ordered for her. "So what happens now?"

"MacKenzie's stay in the U.S. is being extended indefinitely," Michael said with a satisfied gleam in his eye. "His lawyers are scrambling, even going so far as to claim diplomatic immunity. But the truth of the matter is, he is well and truly screwed, even if he does make it back to Scotland. A few of his 'associates' are already cutting deals to save their own asses, and it turns out MacKenzie pissed off a lot of very important people on both sides of the Atlantic."

"Not that I don't already think you're the most amazing man in the world," she told him, "but how did you do it?"

Michael flashed a sexy grin at her, while Lina groaned and rolled her eyes. "Oh, stop," she said to Keely. "His head can barely fit through the door as it is."

Michael crumpled up a napkin and tossed it at his sister. "Just because you're married don't think I can't still put you over my knee," he warned, his voice fierce but his eyes playful.

"I might have a problem with that," Kyle spoke up. Lina looked at him adoringly. At least until he added with a wink, "But I'd be happy to have your back on that one."

"Really, Michael," Stacey said. "How'd you do it?"

"Wasn't that hard, really," he said, shrugging. "Once we got the cousins involved, it was all over for Simon."

"The Callaghans?" Keely asked. She'd met them at the reception, but had been too preoccupied with everything else going on to pay them much attention.

"Yes," Michael confirmed.

"But what do they have to do with anything?"

Michael exchanged a look with his grandfather,

who nodded. "Aye. Tell her. She's part of the family now."

Keely looked from one person to the other. "Tell me what?"

"Let's just say, Uncle Jack and the lads have ways of getting things done outside of official channels."

"Oh. Ooohhhh," she said, catching on.

"I went to Ian when you first disappeared. He used his digital skills to find you, and in doing so, uncovered your true identity. Something didn't sit right with him about Simon, so he started digging deeper and found enough to put him away for a long time. Of course, you provided the final nails for his coffin when you told me what he had done. Sean and Shane paid a visit to the fire marshal who was in charge at the time of the fire. The marshal passed away a few years ago, but they spoke to the son, who confirmed that the marshal had fudged official documents concerning the cause of the blaze."

"Why would he do that?"

"He didn't think he had a choice. The marshal resisted at first. Simon had the son abducted from school to prove a point. The marshal fixed the paperwork the next day in exchange for the safe return of his son. But that's not the most interesting part."

"Oh?"

"Not even close," Michael grinned. "I sketched out your tat for Ian — the *luckenbooth* entwined with a Celtic cross. He ran it through his digital universe and got a few hits."

"It's a family crest," she confirmed.

Conlan smiled. "It's more than just a family crest, lass. Turns out yer mother's family actually has more royal blood than yer father's. As a matter of fact, yer kind of a princess of sorts. Or maybe a duchess. I never really did understand the whole title thing."

Keely nearly choked on her lemonade. "I'm what?"

"They thought the bloodline died out years ago. The women in your family have a long history of getting involved with bad boys from Scotland." Michael's eyes glowed wickedly. "Your great-great-grandmother, the last known heiress, vanished nearly two hundred years ago when she eloped with your great-great-grandfather. The estate's been held in trust indefinitely until an heir could come forward and claim it."

It was too much to take in at once. Stacey was nearly beside herself. "Oh, honey, this is going to make one hell of a story. Assuming you're okay with me penning it, that is."

Keely looked blankly at Stacey in confusion. Lina's eyes opened wide. "Oh my God, that's right! She doesn't know!" Lina turned to Keely. "Keely, Stacey is an author." Her eyes twinkled merrily. "You might have heard of her. She goes by the pen name of Salienne Dulcette."

Keely's mouth gaped as Stacey smiled in confirmation. "Guilty."

Keely turned back to Michael. "Um, would you kiss me, please? Because I simply cannot believe any of this is real." Michael was only too glad to oblige, providing her with a blistering kiss that cleared everything out of her mind for several minutes at least.

"An honest to God heiress, with an aristocratic title," Stacey mused. "You just can't make this stuff up."

"I still can't believe it," Keely said. "I must be dreaming." She looked around the table at her new family, tears forming in her eyes. "How can I ever thank you?"

"You already have, lass, by becoming a part of our family," Conlan beamed. Keely could not stop herself from wrapping her arms around his neck and hugging him fiercely, then placing a kiss on his cheek. There were tears of joy in the old man's eyes.

"Uh-oh," Lina said, narrowing her eyes. "I know that look. What do you know that we don't know, *Daideo*?"

Conlan laughed, his eyes twinkling when he looked at Keely. "Oh, lass, yer going to have yer hands full."

Keely wiped a stray tear from her eye. "Michael's a sweetheart."

"Aye. But he was a real rascal when he was a

wee lad. And those twin boys yer carrying are going to be just like him." He winked and kissed her forehead. Michael looked momentarily stunned, then broke out in a huge grin.

"Twin boys?"

"Aye."

"But how could you possibly know that?" Keely asked, stunned.

"*Daideo* knows things, baby. Just like he knew you were the one for me."

Michael pulled Keely back into his lap, as the others offered their congratulations. Lina laid a comforting hand on her arm, rubbing her round belly with the other. "It's okay, hon. We're all going to get through this together!"

Keely smiled, feeling the love in her heart. For her husband. Her new family.

And her rascals.

Aye, they'd get through it. Together.

Made in United States
Troutdale, OR
09/28/2025